Ahmed Essop

Ahmed Essop was born in 1931. After taking a B.A. degree in 1956 he taught at private schools in Fordsburg. In 1963 he moved to Lenasia where he taught at state schools. In 1974 a succession of transfers ended his teaching career. He worked in commerce for several years and then resumed teaching in Eldorado Park in 1980. In 1986 he left to devote himself to full-time writing. His work includes *The Hajji and Other Stories* (1978), two novels, *The Visitation* (1980) and *The Emperor* (1984), and a further collection of short stories, *Noorjehan and Other Stories* (1990).

The Emperor

Ahmed Essop

Ravan Writers Series

Published by Ravan Press
PO Box 145 Randburg 2125
South Africa

First published in 1984
Second edition 1995
Second impression 1995

ISBN 0 86975 469 6

Cover design: Insight Graphics Pretoria
Cover photograph: Used with the kind permission of *The Star*
                   Johannesburg
Typesetting: Sandy Parker

Acknowledgements:
The poetry of Hafiz reproduced is from *Hafiz, Fifty Poems*, ed A. J.
Arberry, published by Cambridge University Press and that of Jami
from *The Persian Mystics* ed F. Hadland Davis published by Muhammed
Ashraf, Lahore.

All the characters and occurrences in this book are fictional.

Printed by Galvin & Sales, Cape Town
(0605)

For Shehnaaz, Phiroz, Soraya and Zarina

The welfare of the whole world is man's principal duty —
Emperor Ashoka
(286 — 232 B.C.)

CHAPTER ONE

Every year during December, Mr Dharma Ashoka, the vice-principal of the Aryan High School in Lenasia, went down to Durban to sit on the beach and enjoy the sea-breeze that came in off the Indian Ocean. But this year he decided to stay at home, and for a good reason. He had submitted his application to the Education Department — the former principal having retired, the post was now vacant — and felt that anxiety about the outcome of the application would disturb a relaxed mood. It would be a torment to think of the Department's letter lying in his post box in Lenasia.

His decision to stay at home was received with suppressed disappointment by his wife, and vocal disapproval by his thirteen-year-old son, Deva. He tried to pacify Deva by telling him of the important letter he was expecting, and added that if it arrived soon they could still go to Durban. 'You will feel very proud when I am appointed the new principal and you can come with me to school sometimes and help me in the office.'

'But why must the letter spoil our holiday?' Deva asked pettishly.

Mr Ashoka remained silent. Deva would never understand what the letter meant to him: it would bring his career to a consummation.

Mr Ashoka was a tall dark man. From his smooth large forehead receded soft wavy black hair that gathered in glossy curls at the nape of the neck. His grey check suits and white shirts enclosed a body that gave the impression of lean strength, but in reality his muscle fibres were rather feeble. His craggy austere face and long neck were 'classically Dravidian' according to the art teacher at school. His spoken language was fluent; his bearing was confident; his manners at functions were urbane and socially correct. Parents of pupils who met him for the first time were impressed by his appearance and thought him to be a man with personality.

Mr Ashoka was a history teacher. At various times he taught other subjects as well when a teacher was on leave or absent. His pupils found him to be stiff, supercilious and uninspiring. They were afraid to disagree with him. He taught history strictly according to the syllabus and the text-book and accurate reproduction was what he looked for in pupils' essays. When he taught English his emphasis was on formal accuracy rather than the imaginative and creative aspects. He was extremely sparing in awarding marks and was the originator of the practice of giving marks below zero in English composition and the history essay. No pupil ever attempted to make a jest in his presence or even invent a nickname that would fit him. Though he never used the cane to punish pupils, he assailed them verbally with innuendoes and mocking remarks about their performance during tests and examinations. Once he suffered a humiliation that lacerated his psyche for many days. He blamed the principal, Mr Mahara, for it and never forgave him. The school regulation regarding the wearing of the uniform had never been enforced by the principal — whom he regarded as an inefficient administrator — but he decided to enforce it in the two classes he taught. Any pupil not dressed in uniform was told to leave the classroom and forgo the lesson. One day several pupils were banished. The pupils went to look for an empty classroom where they could continue with their studies on their own, but did not find one. It was while they were standing in a corridor that the principal passed by and saw them. He asked them why they were standing there and they explained. Mr Mahara told them to go to the library. Later, he spoke to Mr Ashoka during the tea-break. He told him in a gentle way that although the uniform was an important item of dress at school, it should not lead to the expulsion of pupils from the class. 'There are times, Mr Ashoka,' he said, 'when we are forced not to see things too closely for the sake of our sanity in this disorderly world. Do you remember Horatio's advice to Hamlet in the graveyard? " 'Twere to consider too curiously to consider so." ' Mr Ashoka agreed, but when he went to his class the next day he said angrily, 'From now onwards you can dress like clowns or tramps because you are nothing but clowns and tramps.'

Twice a day he went to the post office, expecting to find the letter appointing him to a position it had been his ambition to reach since he qualified as a teacher. The post at Aryan High School had been denied him when Mr

Mahara had been appointed and several other applications to other schools had been turned down. He recalled his disappointment, but it had been mitigated then by the knowledge that his experience as vice-principal, though attaining the required minimum for promotion, had been insufficient in relation to the experience of other applicants. He could not now be overlooked by the Department as he had been vice-principal for fifteen years. It was a position he had always despised as it was a subordinate one, that of a tiro's, and carried no real authority. During those years he had issued instructions that were within his province and carried out his duties with the efficiency of a functionary. Administrative ability, highly prized by the Department, was essential in running a school and he had cultivated it. In fact Chief Inspector Whitecross, after an inspection of his office work, had said that he considered him to be the most competent person to take over the administration of the school. 'You can rest assured,' he had said, 'that I will recommend you very highly in my report. There is no one with your ability on the Department's horizon. I am certain that you will be considered the most gifted candidate for the post, as well as the Department's most loyal servant.' Filled with elation, he had whispered how grateful he was and assured the inspector of his fealty. He had then dutifully opened the door for him and escorted him to his car. After school he had gone to the stationer, bought an expensive pen set and sent it by post to the inspector with a note saying: 'Thank you very much for your recommendation. Your loyal servant, Dharma Ashoka.'

Besides his experience as vice-principal, he felt that two other factors strongly supported his prospect of being appointed. He had improved his qualifications by private study so that in addition to his Bachelor of Arts degree he had acquired the degrees Bachelor of Arts (Honours) and Bachelor of Education. He was 'triple-degreed', a descriptive phrase he liked to use when among teachers, for it seemed to convey his academic achievements in a forceful way. He was also the president of the Teachers' Association — a position he had surprisingly attained a year before, defeating the previous president who had held office for eight years. He ascribed his victory to his formidable trio of academic achievements which had been publicised in the *Teachers' Chronicle,* the Association's newsletter. The following information had also appeared in his curriculum vitae: 'Mr Ashoka is an official of several organisations, such as Friends of the Blind, the Vedic Society, the Football League, the Chessmen. His mastery of the art of oratory has often been displayed at social functions and teachers' meetings.' During his inaugural presidential address he made this policy statement: 'We as teachers are educationists first and foremost. Our profession forbids us to give anything else priority. Our focus is limited by school boundaries, more specifically by classroom walls. What happens in the outside world of politics and economics is of no concern to us. If we drag the world into the classroom and get embroiled with its concerns the purity of education will be lost. At school we are educationally committed and neutral to all else.'

There had been several occasions at school when some pupils stayed away to take part in political demonstrations. Mr Mahara had never taken action against the pupils. Once, when Mr Ashoka had suggested that they should be re-primanded, Mr Mahara had answered, 'I think we should allow them to do things on their own at times.' He had not expressed his disapproval of this 'highly irresponsible attitude' (as he thought of it) but when the pupils returned to class told them: 'By joining the riff-raff in demonstrations you have broken an unwritten agreement with the school and defied the wishes of your parents who sent you here to be educated. Some of you think you are adults already, you know better than your teachers and can do without them.'

His personal life-style, though not that of an ascetic, was ethical, orderly and controlled: he despised waste, gluttony and sensuality. He considered himself to be 'an eternal student' (a phrase he liked to use in class when deprecating pupils' work) and spoke of man as 'primarily a cognitive being' during academic discussions with teachers. 'Knowledge of the world and the self gives meaning to our existence. Even the Gita recognises this as it speaks of discrimination as life's only purpose.' He knew large tracts of the Gita by heart. 'Not only Muslims have hafiz among them who can recite the Koran from beginning to end. I know the Gita, I am a Hindu hafiz.' He would laugh a little, remaining unaware of the pricked religious sensibility of the Muslim members of his audience.

His relationship towards his wife Sarojini was based on his general principle of orderly existence. He listened to her without interrupting, seldom complained about her cooking, never said a hard word, invariably gave her the house-keeping money on the first day of each month and took her to the sari shop or the jeweller before the approach of festivals. In bed, he used her occasionally and even then briefly. As his wife was a woman taught by religion and her mother to obey her husband, she adapted herself to his pattern of existence with ease.

The days passed and the holidays neared their end and still his post box contained no letter marked 'official'. He began to regret having placed his confidence in the inspector. He regretted buying him the pen set, a thing he had never bought for himself, making do with the cheap ball point pens provided by the Department. It seemed to him that he was going to suffer another humiliation: someone else, perhaps with a single degree, would be appointed principal and he would have to remain in his subordinate position. But three days before the schools reopened the letter lay in his post box. For a moment he did not believe the testimony of his eyes. He looked at it for a while, took a deep breath of relief, and clutching it hurried to his motor-car.

At home he went into his study, tore open the envelope instead of using a stiletto, and read the letter officially appointing him headmaster. Then he went to a book-shelf corner where on a brass tray stood a brass figurine of Lord Krishna. He lit the sacred lamp — a wick in a small red clay bowl — with a match from the tray, joined the palms of his hands and offered a thanksgiving prayer to the god whom he had supplicated for divine assistance in his quest for promotion. He stood there for a long while, the holy light from the wick mantling his face that seemed to be transfigured in beatitude by the certain knowledge of the annunciation contained in the letter. Then he went to the lounge, switched on a tape-recorder and listened to devotional songs and classical Indian music. He was filled with a sense of exaltation which was sustained by the promising horizons that now lay ahead of him in the world of education. He could now reach for an inspector's post, or a rector's post at a teachers' training college, perhaps even the Director of Education's post when it became vacant. He looked at the three frames exhibiting his academic achievements on the lounge wall and saw them as talismans to his future.

At supper time his mood of exaltation subsided a little and he told his family of his preferment. His wife was happy, but not Deva who said:

'If we had gone to Durban the letter would still say the same.'

Mr Ashoka's happiness forbade a quarrel with his son; instead it led him to bestow on Deva five rands and on his wife ten, to spend as they wished.

Before going to bed he read the letter again and it struck him that the Director had used the word headmaster instead of the usual word principal. The word headmaster seemed to carry the connotation that the person in charge of a school was still a teacher, though singled out to administer it. The word principal was not only academically appropriate but radiated the authority of its Latin heritage.

During the next three days Mr Ashoka spent much time in his study where he considered, in a mood of conscious self-importance, how he should administer the school. On one thing he was decided: he would never allow the school to run in the way it had under his predecessor, a weak, lax man who could take firm action against neither insubordinate pupils nor lazy teachers. It was imperative that he made the impress of his authority as soon as possible, for delay could be fatal: so often the rot at a school set in on the very first day and the principal could not regain his authority later. The school must be governed according to a programme devised by him so that in years to come the legacy of his masterly administration would remain, like the lode in auriferous quartz. He began by drafting his inaugural speech to the pupils at assembly; then went on to make a list of provisional rules for pupils to obey, among them the injunction that boys and girls should not communicate with each other during intervals and should keep to their own areas on the playground. He then compiled a preliminary list of restrictions for teachers, beginning with the total prohibition of smoking (although the Department allowed teachers this privilege, he would not). Next he made a tentative list of various changes he intended making in school attendance hours, subject choices, staff, sports activities and so on. He would also take firmer hold of the Parents' Committee and not permit it to have a say in administrative matters as his predecessor had done by consulting them at times and seeking their approval. Their only function was to collect funds for the school and see to its material welfare. Then he turned his attention to the office he was to occupy. Its appearance needed a metamorphosis, for it was the seat of authority and no decree would ever be obeyed if it issued from a mean source. He also briefly considered the idea of changing the name of the school: the word Aryan was not only antiquated but had been debased during the nazi era. There was much for him to accomplish in order to make the school a prestigious one.

CHAPTER TWO

Mr Ashoka's first day as principal was a triumphant one. All the teachers came in the morning to his office to congratulate him, including Mr Saeed who had come over from Pretoria to take over the vacant post of vice-principal. Though no pupils came to congratulate him — perhaps they were awed by his position — he felt happy. Soon, after the exultant ringing of the bell, he would address them. Seated behind a large mahogany table — he was now no longer in the book-room which had served as his office for many years, a room that had been the emblem of his inferior rank — he felt the blood of a heroic conqueror course through his body. His secretary, Mrs Kana, a matronly woman in a peacock-blue sari, consulted him on various minor matters and he smiled and approved. It was not the time to take important decisions and issue orders, but a time to accept compliments, enjoy the honour of holding office, and feel the reality of his authoritative position.

His address to the pupils at assembly was rhetorically delivered: 'As from today I am the principal of this school.' He paused for a moment, then went on: 'I am undertaking my duties with all the seriousness, dedication and responsibility that my position demands. It is a universally accepted fact that a school is not a place of amusement, a pleasure resort, but a place where instruction is given by dedicated teachers to equally dedicated pupils. A school may be compared to an ashram. The teachers are the gurus and the pupils the disciples. There can be no sort of ill-discipline here nor any false ideas about education. You have come to this school of your own free will; therefore, total obedience must be the rule at all times and learning the only end in view. If you have any other intention in coming here, then I want to appeal to you to leave this school now.' He paused again for a moment. 'I am glad no one has been so cowardly as to leave. By remaining you have all freely pledged to learn and to obey. My teachers, I can assure you, will see to that. I want this school to be the finest in the country, a school to be proud of, a school that will have a hundred percent matriculation pass rate every year.'

Mr Ashoka came to the end of his speech and stepped two paces backwards. He then instructed his deputy to take over and order the pupils to march to their classrooms, accompanied by their teachers. A feeling of despondency had come over the pupils and they went quietly.

Mr Ashoka returned to his office. Outside, new pupils accompanied by their parents were waiting to be enrolled. Mr Ashoka sent his secretary to call Mr Saeed. When he came he instructed him to enrol the pupils in the school hall, and added: 'After you have done, please keep all the parents in the hall as I wish to address them.' Mr Saeed, a short, light-complexioned, corpulent man whose head was an ellipsoid covered with dense curly brown hair, listened to his superior with his head bowed and then left to carry out the duty entrusted to him.

Various teachers came to consult Mr Ashoka. Ostensibly they came on some matter (had the matriculation textbooks been changed? or had the epidiascope been repaired?) but in reality they came to demonstrate their recognition of him as their superior. The first to enter the office was the senior science teacher. Before Mr Mahara's time he had regarded the laboratory as his private circle in Inferno. There the crucible, the tong, the battery, the clamps and the bunsen burner, so many instruments of torture, had lent scope to his imprisoned psyche. In penance for these former cruelties, during Mr Mahara's time he had undergone a transformation and made the laboratory his monastery, where he spent many hours assembling apparatus for the next day's experiments and meticulously correcting pupils' note-books. He was followed by the sportsmaster, a flamboyantly-dressed dwarf in purple suit, rose pink shirt, polka-dotted tie, whose zealot's love for exercise infected even the most lethargic of youth and made them perform extraordinary acrobatic feats. The next to enter was the accounting teacher, a man who seemed to have swelled into the shape of a prosperous merchant by tabulating theoretical business deals. The mathematics teacher was a geometrical wraith. so pale and linear he looked. The history teacher unshakably believed that there was a conspiracy to denigrate his subject as it was not compulsory in the curriculum. He took revenge — he was the stock-controller — by withholding from the other teachers their complete requisitions, thus earning for himself the jibe, 'Keeper of the Crown Jewels'. Last came the biology teacher, a bearded man who spoke at school of the virtues of coeducation, and in the mosque (he was a priest, too) of the ancient wisdom of keeping girls at home.

Later Mr Saeed came to call Mr Ashoka to address the parents. His address — an oration on 'the importance of the school in the intellectual life of the community' and 'the importance of learning to grow into full human beings' ended: 'Ladies and gentlemen, let us work together to bring light — a sacred word in our Hindu religion — to our children. Let us not be found wanting, for the judgement of history is of all judgements the most terrible.'

In the afternoon, Mr Ashoka asked his secretary for the log book which was kept in a safe in the brick-built strong-room (the entire school was a structure of pre-fabricated asbestos panels) whose massive steel door was directly behind his office chair. He made the following entry: 'I assumed duty as principal of Aryan High School today. The day was spent in reorganisational and administrative activities.'

After handing back the book to his secretary he felt so grateful to Dr Whitecross and the Director of Education for his promotion that he decided he would extend at the end of the year a special invitation to them to visit the school. It would be a great festive day — all the parents and pupils would be present — and after a thanksgiving speech he would garland the distinguished guests on the stage in the school hall.

Next morning, Dr Raj, chairman of the school's Parents' Committee, telephoned Mr Ashoka and congratulated him on his appointment.

'Thank you very much, Dr Raj,' Mr Ashoka replied. 'I expected a visit from your committee yesterday so that parents, pupils and teachers could see that you are interested in education.'

'Mr Ashoka, it is difficult for me to get the committee members together without prior notice because of business . . . .'

'Then they should not be on the committee. Their obligations to the school come first.'

'Mr Ashoka, we shall come to the school as soon as we can,' Dr Raj said apologetically, not wishing to get involved in an argument with the new principal.

'I suppose it's a case of better late than never,' Mr Ashoka said with ironic emphasis.

Dr Raj telephoned the members of the committee and as soon as he could get away from his surgery picked them up in his car and drove to the school. Mr Ashoka had audience with them in his office. Dr Raj, a tall man with a hazelnut brown forehead, wearing rimless spectacles and the usual doctor's white outfit, formally congratulated Mr Ashoka and said that the committee was pleased he had been appointed and not someone else from another school. 'I am sure we shall be able to work happily together for many years,' he concluded.

Mr Ashoka then addressed them: 'Gentlemen, you will appreciate that every man has his own views about the education of school children. But in this world not everybody's views can be accepted and put into practice. We should leave it to those who are most competent. Now, my predecessor was an able man, you will agree, but my views are different from his. Discipline was not one of his strong points. You are all aware of the first principle of the Hindu religion — it is discipline. This is most important in the process of education, despite the fancy ideas of modern educationists, and I have made a study of all of them. I intend to exact discipline from the pupils of this school and I hope that you will give me your co-operation.'

Dr Raj said that he and his committee would do everything to help.

'Now, gentlemen,' Mr Ashoka went on, 'I am sure you will appreciate that my predecessor was not particular about appearances, for instance the appearance of this office. You will agree that the furniture and fittings are in no way a credit to this school, nor to you. When people visit this school they should be impressed.'

Dr Raj turned to the treasurer, Mr Ismail, and asked him if the committee had enough funds in the bank.

'Yes,' he answered, 'fortunately we spent little last year.'

'I leave the matter to you, gentlemen,' Mr Ashoka said, rising from his chair.

Shortly after the committee had left, Dr Whitecross's secretary telephoned to say that the inspector would be visiting the school the next day.

As soon as the inspector's car came to a halt outside the school gate Mr Ashoka was informed by a servant, who had been stationed there since the morning to watch for the arrival of a white Ford. Mr Ashoka hurried out of his office, after telling several parents — to whom he had delivered a lecture on delinquent children in the community and expounded his theory of education based on discipline — that they should leave the school premises by the rear gate as he was about to receive a 'very important educationist' at the front gate.

'Good morning, Dr Whitecross,' Mr Ashoka said, opening the door of the car and shaking his hand as he emerged. 'The entire school is waiting for your arrival.'

The inspector smiled. Mr Ashoka took his briefcase and the two men walked along the flower-skirted pathway to the office.

Dr Whitecross was a tall man with a bone-revealing face, his dark grey eyes like shells under river water. His complexion was a mottled white. He was invariably dressed in a sombre grey suit and a spotless white shirt, even when invited to attend a school's sports day.

The inspector was surprised at the silence which shrouded the school. Mr Ashoka had sent out a note to all teachers early that morning urging them 'to exercise the sternest measures' against pupils who talked on that day. As the inspector was coming it was 'imperative that the entire school make a good impression upon him.'

As soon as the inspector was seated in the office the secretary, in a flamingo-red sari, brought tea and biscuits.

After she had left, Mr Ashoka closed the door and said, 'Dr Whitecross, I want to thank you for the strong recommendation of my abilities to the Department. I am obligated to you for the rest of my life.'

'You deserve the post,' the inspector said. 'I think you are going to achieve great things.'

'God willing,' Mr Ashoka said. 'With your help I shall make this school the finest in the country.'

'You are the right person for that,' the inspector said. 'You know I have great respect for the Indian race. You are such hard-working people.'

'Thank you very much.'

'Now to turn to official matters,' Dr Whitecross said, taking a writing pad from his bag, 'what is the roll of your school?'

'At present it is nine hundred and twelve.'

'Your staff?'

'Thirty-seven teachers; twenty-seven males and ten females. Seven males are graduates and five are expected to complete their degrees at the end of this year. Two females are graduates and two will start studying for their degrees this year. There is one unqualified female teacher.'

'You have all the facts at your fingertips,' Dr Whitecross commended, writing with the pen given to him by Mr Ashoka. 'I am sure we are going to see a great deal of progress at this school.'

When Dr Whitecross had finished — he had only recorded the roll and the number of teachers without the other details — he put his writing pad into his bag and was ready to leave.

'I have to visit many schools today,' he said, rising from his chair.

'Dr Whitecross,' Mr Ashoka said, standing deferentially before his superior, 'please accept an invitation to lunch. My wife and I would be honoured to entertain your whole family.'

'My wife and I have no children,' Dr Whitecross said. 'But I shall be happy to accept the invitation.'

Mr Ashoka mentioned a Sunday, wrote down his home address on a sheet of paper, and handed it to the inspector.

'Dr Whitecross,' Mr Ashoka said, as they walked out of the office, 'would you mind visiting one class before you go — just to see how we are getting on?'

'I don't have much time, but . . . all right.'

Mr Ashoka led the inspector to a classroom near his office. During the holidays the asbestos panels of this particular classroom had been cunningly painted by the teacher to look like stone-work. The inspector approved of what the teacher had done and commented, 'The teacher in this class shows us what can be done if we use our imaginations properly.'

'He is a mathematics teacher,' Mr Ashoka informed him, knocking at the door and opening it for the inspector to enter.

The teacher stopped teaching. The pupils stood up and greeted the visitors.

'Carry on with your lesson, Mr Pillay,' Mr Ashoka said in a commanding voice. 'We shall stand at the back and listen.'

The teacher had drawn a triangle on the board and went on to prove that the three angles made up 180 degrees.

'Thank you very much,' the inspector said when the teacher had finished. 'That was a very good lesson.'

The visitors took their leave of the pupils and left the room.

Outside, as the two men walked towards the car, Dr Whitecross said, 'It is amazing how you have managed to get the school organised in a few days. Lessons have commenced. Usually schools take a week or two to settle down. They will have to catch up with your school in future.'

'I have some very co-operative members on my staff. They have worked late into the night to complete the time-tables.'

'I shall make a note of that,' the inspector said, getting into his car.

Truthfully Mr Ashoka could have said that he had worked late into the night on the time-tables himself. But he wished to create the larger impression of his administrative ability, rather than stressing his own individual capacity for work.

CHAPTER THREE

On Monday morning a furniture dealer's van arrived and shortly afterwards an interior decorator was followed by a carpet dealer's assistant. Within several hours Mr Ashoka's office was transformed: it lost its bureaucratic sombreness (how heavy the old table and chairs were, as though they carried the weight of past years!) to the brittle dash of a modern business executive's office where cigars are smoked and profit and loss accounts examined. Mr Ashoka was very satisfied with the change, for his office now projected not only his authority but his ability to command material resources. And it was while he was sitting in his new chair that his eyes fell on the framed photograph of his predecessor standing among a number of teachers. The photograph had an aged yellowed look like those to be seen among bric-à-brac in a second-hand dealer's shop. Mr Ashoka saw a youthful version of himself standing in the rear, an insignificant saturnine figure. Suddenly shame and anger seized him: shame at the many years it had taken him, years of ambition-driven study and slavish abasement to his superiors, to reach his present position; and anger at his predecessor for having had supremacy over him. He rose impulsively from his chair, went towards the wall where the photograph was hanging and unhooked it. Then he walked out with it to a storeroom and flung it in a corner among rolls of dusty drawing paper. The glass shattered and the frame buckled. A sense of elation filled him. He would destroy everything that reminded him of the reign of his predecessor. He would erase everything that could in any way be considered as part of the history of the school.

The next day he summoned a meeting of the Parents' Committee and said to them: 'According to circular RX 343 it is your prerogative, should you wish, to change the name of the school. Now this school is named after an ancient race that entered India some time in the twelfth century B.C. To me this name is meaningless in these modern times, if not absurd. I want the school renamed and I suggest that you rename it as the Ashoka High School in honour of the great Indian emperor who reigned in the third century B.C.'

There was silence for a while.

'Some of you seem to have reservations,' Mr Ashoka went on, 'because my name happens to be the same as the emperor's, but you will appreciate that that is merely accidental. You should have no hesitation in making the change. Incidentally, some historians spell the emperor's name without the letter "h".'

'We will consider the matter and let you know tomorrow,' Dr Raj said.

'I want a decision now,' Mr Ashoka said firmly.

'If any members of the Parents' Committee have objections,' Dr Raj said, 'please let me hear them.'

No one spoke.

'In that case we agree to the change.'

'Now,' Mr Ashoka said, 'I don't want a sign-board similar to the one outside. I want a granite slab of three metres by two, with the letters in marble; this to be placed on a foundation of brickwork two metres high. The change in name will also involve a change in the uniform and the monogram of the pupils. I shall decide on the colours and inform the pupils. There will also be several other minor adjustments because of the change, but you can leave that to me.'

The Parents' Committee left, feeling helpless. They could not antagonise Mr Ashoka, who was vested with governmental authority, but on the other hand they were answerable to parents for decisions taken and moneys spent. The erection of the granite slab and the change in uniform would involve considerable expense and they could find themselves accused of being pawns in Mr Ashoka's hands.

After a week the brick foundation was completed and the stone-masons arrived to position the slab, using pulleys. Several teachers and pupils stood nearby to watch. When they saw the new name of the school — Mr Ashoka had not told anyone of the change, as everyone would soon see it in marble — there was some laughter and amusement. More teachers and pupils gathered.

Mr Ashoka heard the commotion from his office and looked out of the window. Stung by their laughter, his first impulse was to rush outside and tell everyone that he saw nothing amusing about a change in name, and that only the simple-minded would find it so. He sent his secretary to call Mr Saeed. When his deputy came he said to him, 'Please go and tell all those teachers and pupils standing near the front gate watching the positioning of the slab to disperse immediately.' Mr Saeed went out and Mr Ashoka watched from the window. The teachers then regrouped in a circle a short distance away.

When Mr Saeed returned to the office, Mr Ashoka said to him, 'You have seen the new name of the school. It is now named after the great Indian emperor who reigned in the third century B.C. It is an accident that the name happens to be the same as mine.'

Mr Saeed, totally ignorant of Indian history, did not comment, afraid to display his ignorance to his superior.

'I objected when the Parents' Committee suggested the change,' Mr Ashoka continued. 'It is embarrassing, but what can I do. Please go and explain to all the pupils and teachers.'

'I think the Parents' Committee did the right thing,' Mr Saeed said, and left to carry out his instruction.

Mr Ashoka then sat down at his table and wrote two letters: one to the Department and one to Dr Whitecross informing them of the Parents' Committee's decision to change the name of the school. But while writing the letters he remembered the laughter of the teachers and felt riled. When he went home he sat down in his study and thought what he should do to assert his authority with greater force. He realised that he needed the assistance of others besides his deputy: divide and rule. There were several teachers — he had seen two of them with the group Mr Saeed had attempted to disperse — who would always look for opportunities to voice their cynicism against legitimate authority; motivated by jealousy, maliciousness and egotism, they could become a threat to him by instigating others to disobedience. He would counter them by establishing a Disciplinary Committee consisting only of the mathematics and science teachers, and delegate certain powers to them.

The next day he called the teachers to his office and said: 'Gentlemen, I have especially sent for you as I intend establishing a Disciplinary Committee to assist me and the vice-principal in maintaining law and order in this school. By temperament, training and by virtue of the subjects you teach, which are strictly empirical, I consider you to be the most suitable persons to be vested with disciplinary authority. Mr Saeed will now issue to you a roneoed copy of the terms of reference of your authority.'

After the copies were given out Mr Ashoka began reading: '(a) Members of the Disciplinary Committee shall position themselves in the morning in front of the school gates and close them as soon as the bell rings. Pupils who are late shall be kept out, their names recorded, and afterwards marched to the vice-principal's office to be punished as the Committee deems fit. (b) During playtimes and assemblies you shall exercise strict control. (c) Not only during school hours but at all times the Committee shall exercise vigilance and prevent any pupil or teacher from bringing disrepute to the school. (d) If any rude or undisciplined parents or members of the community come to this school with a view to causing a disturbance, or act in an undignified way that may bring disorder or disgrace to the school, they shall be summarily ejected by the Committee. If necessary, call the police. (e) All forms of disobedience, immoral conduct, delinquency, disgraceful behaviour, truancy, insubordination, sedition, shall be ruthlessly stamped out. (f) The Committee shall not permit any smoking, drug-taking or alcohol consumption on school premises by pupils. (g) The Committee shall assist the principal and vice-principal at all times in the exercise of authority, control, order and good administration. (h) The head of the Committee shall be the vice-principal, who will refer all disciplinary matters to the principal if and when necessary.'

Mr Ashoka was silent when he had finished. He wanted to hear if the teachers had anything to say, then smiled when no one said a word. 'Gentlemen, I am proud of your loyalty to me and the school in undertaking the duties entrusted to you. I would have you note clause (c) of the terms of your authority very carefully. We cannot permit any person or persons to undermine authority or act in such a way as to be disloyal. Depending on the way you execute your duties, I shall submit favourable reports to the Department. Needless to say, my reports will play a vital role in your future prospects of promotion in the teaching profession.'

Later, in the afternoon, Mr Ashoka went home and returned with a large gilt-framed photograph of himself. He hung it on the wall opposite his chair.

CHAPTER FOUR

At his home in Gardenia Street, Mr Ashoka waited nervously for Dr Whitecross and his wife to arrive, making periodic visits to the kitchen to see if the cooking had been completed and to the dining-room to see if the maid was arranging the crockery and cutlery properly. He was going to entertain a very important government official and he wanted all the preparations made before his arrival. Besides, Dr Whitecross had been instrumental in his promotion and he wanted to show him his gratitude.

But one anxiety afflicted Mr Ashoka's mind — his son Deva. The boy had been a disappointment to him since the day he began school. He believed that he was mentally retarded, if not quite an imbecile. He had done everything he could for him once the boy had mastered the ability to use a pen, but Deva had failed to grasp the simplest of lessons. Even elementary arithmetical problems had been beyond his understanding. He had spent many hours with him in his study, patiently going over the rudiments and explaining the lessons ten times over, but to no avail. He had used all the approaches to learning he had been taught during his training college days, from the traditional disciplinarian's way, which he considered to be the soundest, to the 'play' way as prescribed by modern educationists, but the boy had defied everything in the manuals of instruction. He had even consulted a psychologist by telephone, but had been afraid to take Deva for an examination in case the psychologist confirmed his fears. The boy was now in Standard Three, having spent two years in each previous standard. If he went on in this way he would be twenty-five years old by the time he matriculated. This terrifying possibility had hardened Mr Ashoka, and he had severely limited Deva's recreation. Even now the boy was in the study writing a composition on the topic, 'A day in the life of a farmer'. Mr Ashoka knew that the composition would never be completed even if his son remained in the study the whole day and was capable of expressing himself in grammatically and syntactically correct English. He knew that if he went into the study he would find Deva playing with paper planes, or spinning the globe (which he had bought to show him, among others things, the Greenwich meridian) at a speed that threatened to dislocate it from its pivots and send it flying through the open window; or he would be looking at the pictures in an encyclopaedia instead of reading and assimilating information; or wasting his time drawing. Deva had a talent for drawing; but Mr Ashoka knew it was a worthless activity indulged in by freaks and bohemians. In any case who had ever heard of an Indian artist?

Now that the inspector was coming Mr Ashoka was faced with a problem. If he kept the boy locked up during the inspector's visit he might start kicking at the door and making strange hooting sounds that might give the inspector the impression that there was something sinister going on in his house; if he allowed him out he might say things that could embarrass him and his guest. In any case dinner was usually a family affair on Sundays and if he did not ask Deva to join them the boy might work himself into a tantrum and start breaking things. He decided that his best course was to speak to Deva and tell him that a very important man was coming to have dinner with them and that he should show him how well Indians, who were a very civilized race, behaved.

Deva, a physically stunted boy with a small forehead and a mop of thick glossy black hair which his mother loved to smear with coconut oil and comb every morning, grinned and said:

'I always behave in class when the inspector comes.'

'That's very good,' his father said. 'And when we are having dinner do not speak at all and listen to what he says.'

'I always behave in class when the inspector comes,' Deva repeated, grinning mischievously and jumping up and down.

When the visitors arrived Mr Ashoka went to the front gate to welcome them. Dr Whitecross was dressed in a faintly-striped charcoal suit and his wife — a fat-burdened, gentle, soprano-voiced woman — in a suit patterned with brown checks. Heavily made-up and excessively perfumed, she smiled pleasantly at Mr Ashoka.

The visitors were led into the house where they were introduced to Mrs Ashoka and Deva. Mrs Ashoka was dressed in a marine-blue sari elaborately bordered in gold.

Her red bodice held her burnt-sienna bosom very tightly. Her face was round and her sparse hair drawn backwards and coiled into a bun. Mrs Ashoka shook hands and smiled. Deva gave his hand to the guests and the inspector put his hand on his shoulder and said, 'I am sure the son is as clever as the father.'

Mr Ashoka looked apprehensively at Deva, but when the boy remained quiet and only looked at the visitors, he smiled and said, 'Only time will tell.'

'Time waits for no boy,' Deva said.

'Brilliant boy!' Dr Whitecross said, patting him on the shoulder.

They all went into the lounge and sat down for some small talk. Mr Ashoka and Dr Whitecross had some whisky. Deva sat beside the inspector and gazed at him silently, which reassured his father.

After a while the maid, in Mrs Ashoka's cast-off sari, came to announce that dinner was served. After the meal was over, the ladies went into an inner room — Mrs Ashoka wanted to show her guest some of her embroidery — and the two men and Deva went to the lounge.

'You know, Mr Ashoka,' Dr Whitecross said, 'for some time now I have been thinking of introducing in our primary schools something similar to Differential Education in our high schools. For instance, we could have all the bright children in one group, say in the A class; the average ones in another, the B class; and the weaker ones in the C class. What do you think of my idea?'

'I think it is a very good idea.'

'I wanted your approval as president of the Teachers' Association before trying it out. If your Association supports me I shall be very pleased. You know there are always some people who are opposed to anything new.'

'I know in which class I will be,' Deva said to the inspector.

Dr Whitecross was taken aback for a moment as though the boy had challenged the educational worth of his idea. But he recovered quickly and said, 'You will be in the A class.'

'Wrong!' Deva replied. 'I will be in my own class!'

'Your own class?' Dr Whitecross asked quizzically.

'Yes, because I am cleverer than anyone else!'

'Deva,' Mr Ashoka said, maintaining his composure, 'we are discussing something very important. Dr Whitecross, please carry on.'

'It is an educational concept in line with modern thought. Of course at primary level we shall not be able to provide practical courses for the weaker ones as we do in our high schools. Under my system the gifted pupils will progress without being held back by the stupid ones, or the less clever ones . . . .'

'That means the same,' Deva said.

The inspector smiled at him and went on speaking. 'The less clever ones will also be advantaged. The teacher will be able to understand them better and work harder with them . . . .'

'He may become cross and beat them,' Deva commented.

'It is bad manners to interrupt,' Mr Ashoka said, for a moment losing his composure and looking annoyed. Dr Whitecross went on speaking.

'As in our high schools, the best teachers will teach the clever pupils . . . .'

'The clever pupils can teach themselves,' Deva said with a sagacious look on his face. 'The best teachers should teach the less clever pupils.'

'Keep quiet!' Mr Ashoka said, desperately restraining his anger. Deva put his finger to his lips.

'If you support my idea through your Teachers' Association it will be of great help. I shall soon instruct primary school principals to put the system into operation. After all, separation is to be found everywhere in nature. The fittest get the best. Why shouldn't the clever pupils get the best education?'

'I fully agree,' Mr Ashoka said. 'Indian civilisation also believes in differentiation. There are the various castes.'

'Thank you very much. I am reminded of your wonderful defence of Differential Education at your teachers' conference a few years ago when you answered the critics. I remember it well. You said that Christ probably started Differential Education when he said, "In my Father's house are many mansions." That was a brilliant answer. Do you know that I informed the Department of what you said and you gained a plus mark?'

'I am grateful,' Mr Ashoka said.

'I only want to do my best for the Indian child,' Dr Whitecross went on. 'Under my system the bright child will be isolated at an early age and society will know its future professors, doctors and lawyers, and those who will do other kinds of work . . . . '

'Such as teachers and inspectors,' Deva shouted, jumping up and running round the room.

Mr Ashoka stood up, fuming. Deva ran out of the room.

'Sit down,' Dr Whitecross said to his host. 'Don't trouble yourself. I understand children.'

'I should have sent him to the cinema,' Mr Ashoka said.

'Do they have cinema shows on Sundays here?' Dr Whitecross asked.

'No, of course not. I forgot for a moment.'

'I think you have a very bright son, Mr Ashoka. I am sure he is going to outstrip the father some day.'

Mr Ashoka had no wish to talk about his son. He asked instead, 'Will the Department support you in implementing the system?'

'As long as you get your Teachers' Association to support it I will get the Department's support.'

'I will do my best for you at the next meeting,' Mr Ashoka promised his superior.

'I know I can rely on you,' Dr Whitecross said thankfully.

'Tell me Dr Whitecross,' Mr Ashoka enquired, changing the course of the conversation, 'what was the title of your doctoral thesis?'

'I called it "A Study of Syllabus Patterns in Indian Schools and a Critique of Pedagogical Approaches to Racial and Cultural Differentiation".'

'So you are an expert on Indian education?'

'Otherwise I would not hold the post of chief inspector.'

'Dr Whitecross, are you familiar with the history of India? Especially the reign of the great emperor Ashoka?'

'I regret I am not. But he must have been a very clever man, to judge from his namesake.'

'Well, he reigned during the Third Century B.C.'

'He must have been something like our State President who is a very wise man. Do you know that our State President was a teacher before he was called to parliament to serve the nation as its head?'

'I didn't know that.'

'Yes, if he had not been called by destiny to make greater sacrifices for the nation he would today have been a great figure in education.'

'I am sure he would,' Mr Ashoka agreed. 'You know the emperor Ashoka is one of the great figures in the history of the world.'

'Our president, I can assure you, will go down in history when all the emperors of the past primitive ages are forgotten, and mainly because he was once a teacher.'

Deva came back into the room and sat down beside the inspector. He had tied a red band around his head in which he had stuck two green feathers.

'Run along, Deva, and play in the garden,' his father advised him.

'No, not today. Last year the inspector came to our class and when he left the teacher said . . . . '

'What did he say?' the inspector asked quickly.

'You are the biggest fool on earth.'

Mr Ashoka withered. Dr Whitecross asked calmly: 'Deva, good boy, tell me: which school do you attend, and what is your teacher's name?'

'I won't tell you because you will go and bully my sir,' Deva answered defiantly. 'And if you are the biggest fool on earth then my father can't say that I am the biggest fool on earth.'

Deva leapt into the air, fell on the carpet, rolled over, jumped up and ran yelling out of the room.

CHAPTER FIVE

The next day Mr Ashoka was ready to hold, in the words he used to Mr Saeed, 'the first plenary staff meeting at Ashoka High School'. The Disciplinary Committee had now been established and he could count on its support against teachers who opposed his views. His confidence led him to put on his graduation gown which he had brought with him in a bag from home. He then sent out his secretary with a notice summoning all teachers to the staffroom.

The teachers gathered with a sense of expectancy. Some had already perceived that Mr Ashoka had undergone a personality change since his appointment as principal. He seemed to have assumed the manner and disposition of a potentate. The changed office, with its imposing modernity, and the change in the name of the school, with the implausible explanation about the commemoration of an ancient emperor's name, were to them the objective manifestations of a man who would be Caesar. The first staff meeting was always crucial for teachers, as it gave them the opportunity to gauge the way in which the new principal intended to run the school, and to work out their own attitude and approach to him. They received their first surprise when Mr Saeed announced, 'Ladies and gentlemen, please take the chairs allocated to you as shown on the labels at the back of each chair.'

There was some confusion as teachers had never heard of such a novel arrangement and queried its purpose. There was some laughter when Mrs Zenobia Hansa, the new English teacher, said that the staff-room was now being elevated to the status of the General Assembly hall at U.N. headquarters. After five minutes Mr Ashoka entered, followed by Mr Saeed carrying several files. Their entry had an air of theatricality, the begowned Mr Ashoka looking like a judge in a play. Some of the teachers were surprised and others amused. The wearing of an academic gown in Lenasia was unprecedented. The two men went to a table in front.

'Ladies and gentlemen,' Mr Ashoka began, 'those of you who are alert will by now have deduced what sort of tone I intend setting in administering this school — one of absolute order and control. I have already spoken in my inaugural address on the theme of discipline which I regard as the hallmark of every civilised individual. There was a great deal of laxity at this school during the past and I shall have none of it now, from teacher or pupil. The allocation of specific seats to you at this staff meeting demonstrates the sort of order I want. Will everyone please check now whether they are seated in the chairs allocated to them.'

All the teachers rose to examine their names written on strips of yellow paper and fixed with transparent tape.

There was some confusion as some teachers had been allocated more than one chair. There was laughter.

'Who is responsible for this anomaly?' Mr Ashoka asked angrily. He stood up impulsively and glared at the teachers as though there was a conspiracy to demean his dignity and authority.

'Sir,' Mr Saeed explained, 'I asked some pupils to assist me in writing the names of the teachers, and they may have perpetrated the error.'

'Then find out the culprits immediately after this meeting and punish them,' Mr Ashoka said, sitting down in his chair. 'And ask responsible pupils to assist you in future,' he added. Mr Saeed bowed his head in what seemed like contrition.

'Now,' Mr Ashoka continued, 'to prove my point about laxity in the past I want to draw your attention to last year's matriculation examination results. My analysis shows that eighty-two percent of the pupils who wrote the examination passed. To some of you this may seem satisfactory, but as far as I am concerned it is putrid. Under my administration this school must produce a hundred percent pass every year — otherwise you are failing in your duty as teachers and not earning your monthly salaries. Remember that you are being paid from public funds — the government merely administers these — and if pupils fail then you are guilty of defrauding the public. I have spent several nights going over the examination results and my analysis shows that some pupils in the present matriculation class were promoted on the basis of probability rather than certainty of making the grade. In other words some pupils were promoted by teachers on criteria other than academic merit. I am in the process of looking at the mark records and shall soon announce the names of pupils to be demoted from the matriculation class. No dead wood shall be permitted to write the matriculation examination.'

There was a murmur of disapproval from some teachers, but Mr Ashoka went on, 'This may seem unprecedented to some of you, but it must be understood that I am fully responsible for all decisions taken and shall not tolerate objections from teachers, parents or the Parents' Committee.

'There are several other matters I want to bring to your attention at this stage. Teachers seem to think they can come to school whenever they wish. I want all teachers to report for duty twenty minutes before the morning bell and remain at school twenty minutes after the final bell. Teachers who arrive late must immediately submit a report in triplicate giving their reasons for being late.

'Now I want to go on to the very important matter of keeping adequate records. All teachers must possess for each subject a file in which there shall be a typed copy of the prescribed official syllabus; a detailed scheme of work for the year divided into four terms and making reference to all the text-books and reference books to be consulted; a daily record of all lessons delivered under the sub-headings subject matter, method of presentation, apparatus used and pupil activity. These records shall be submitted to the senior teachers, that is the subject departmental heads, and they in turn shall submit the records to me every Friday. Any teacher who fails to submit these records shall be subject to disciplinary action. I shall also visit classrooms periodically and listen to lessons.

'In order to maintain discipline I have appointed a Disciplinary Committee to assist me in my task. The

Committee consists of the mathematics and science teachers. I have especially selected them as they are involved in the teaching of the exact subjects and appreciate the values of discipline, order, control and obedience. They are opposed to anarchy, as I am. This Committee shall deal with all disciplinary problems.'

Mr Ashoka's revelation was received with silent indignation. Teachers who were excluded from the Committee were shocked at the clandestine manner in which it had been formed. They realised that Mr Ashoka had cunningly divided the staff in order to hold sway over them. Some felt that the mathematics and science teachers had displayed bad faith, if not downright treachery, by allowing themselves to be deceived by Mr Ashoka's flattery and spurious reasoning.

'For the promotion of efficient administration,' Mr Ashoka continued, his voice lifted to a haughty mandarin register, 'no pupil or teacher shall come to see me without the authority of the vice-principal, who will consider whether the matter merits my attention or not, and on the same basis no pupil shall see the vice-principal without the consent of the teacher. I do not wish to concern myself with trivialities.

'In conclusion, I wish to reiterate my statement to the pupils at assembly on the first day when the school re-opened. I said that the pupils had freely chosen to come to this school and must obey. You, too, have freely chosen to be here and I expect you to obey. If any of you dislike the way in which I intend to administer my school, you are at liberty to leave and you should do so now. I want teachers who are loyal to me, teachers who will spend their time and energies — remember that your contract stipulates that you are at the service of the Department twenty-four hours of the day — in what I am engaged in — the education of the Indian child. I am an educationist first and foremost, and whatever I do is in the cause of education.'

With that final theatrical sentence Mr Ashoka stood up to leave the staffroom, but was prevented when Zenobia asked if she might be permitted to say a few words.

'Yes,' Mr Ashoka said, sitting down, 'provided that what you want to say is something general. I cannot permit you to give your opinion on any matter that lies within the field of my authority and responsibility.'

'All I wish to say at this stage, Mr Ashoka,' Zenobia said, 'is that the school is a public institution. You seem to be under the impression that it belongs to you.'

Mr Ashoka rose from his seat, rage strangling his vocal chords. Then he walked out of the room, followed dutifully by Mr Saeed.

The teachers remained in their seats for a while, saying nothing. Challenging the head of a school was unheard of, for the head was a powerful man, backed by a formidable phalanx of inspectors, the Education Department, the Minister of Education and ultimately the government.

CHAPTER SIX

Zenobia was tall, with long black hair and a Nefertiti profile. Her eyes were amber in colour, warm and bright under dusky eye-lids. She had a flair for selecting clothing to adorn her erect slender body, and whether she wore a sari, a kaftan, a sarong, a tunic with flowing pants, or a skirt and blouse, with matching bangles, brooches, rings and pendants, her harmoniously colourful form always reflected her serene personality.

She had taught for many years at a private school in Fordsburg before coming to live and take a teacher's post in Lenasia. A naturally happy woman, she enjoyed teaching children. She was always ready with kind words for those who failed to appreciate or understand fully. She attempted to inspire in her pupils a love of literature, whether drama, poetry or prose. Her eclectic mind made her range beyond the prescribed play, poem or novel to other literatures and cultures, from ancient Greece, to Persia, to India, to China. The education of children, to Zenobia, was an infinitely complex activity. No pupil was a tablet or anaesthetised object; each one was a concentration of personal, social, cultural and historical tissues, living in a specific time and place, determined by the flux of contemporary social, economic and political forces. She believed that pupils should be made aware of the forces that shaped their lives. She wanted her pupils to think for themselves, to give their own opinions even if these were wrong, to be critical and argumentative, to appraise and weigh, to write and speak freely without fear, to learn to make decisions and choices after consideration. She also wanted them to be imaginative and creative. She believed that the educative process should be a joy and end in itself; it should be an extension of the happiness with which children were endowed at birth. The mere gathering of information and the year-end internment in an examination room she considered to be destructive of the delicate psyche of pupils. Pre-eminently, she considered the school to be the place for the cultivation and refinement of human sensibilities.

At Ashoka High School Zenobia quickly came to perceive that the whole approach to education differed radically from her own. Here education was formalised and institutionalised by a hierarchy of teachers, with the principal as the chief hierarch. Here the preoccupation was with achievement scores in examinations, and the important values were obedience, respect, hard work, correctness of reproduction, knowledge of facts. The emphasis of the entire system was on the semantics of the literal, rather than on the abstract, the conceptual, figurative, inferential, symbolic, intentional, emotive. Looked upon as raw material to be shaped in terms of the curricula, the pupils were left derelict when it came to meeting the forces that moulded their lives. Beneath the system lay the authoritarian ideology of politicians, the dogmas of race and nation and state. Teachers, working under the system, became subtly infected and projected attitudes that were static, authoritarian and final.

Zenobia soon came to realise that she could never accept a system that negated everything she believed in. In Mr Ashoka she saw a bureaucratic tyrant, fulsomely conceited, his mind beginning to calcify with power and position. He was not only removed from warm human relationships with pupils and teachers, but from all that reflected good taste and sensitivity. She had passed his home on several occasions and had not been surprised to find it painted ochre and deep blue, not a flower or tree growing on the small patch of lawn in front. Should she pity him? Should she try to reason with him? This she realised would be useless, for men of tyrannical disposition often mistook gentleness and understanding, even courtesy, as expressions of fear and servility, gratifying their pride and power. She would oppose him, she decided: he and all those who supported him.

Zenobia's husband, Kamar, was an advocate, a man of outstanding academic achievement who had gained fame by his defence of people arraigned for political crimes. In an age when advocates were notorious for the exorbitant fees they commanded for their services, his charges were moderate — and there were clients from whom he would accept nothing at all. Kamar and Zenobia had two daughters at university. They had adopted two others, a boy and a girl, who were attending primary school. In Fordsburg, their home had always been a gathering place for people of varying pursuits and interests;

even now in Lenasia, during weekends, they had many visitors.

CHAPTER SEVEN

For many days Zenobia's words at the staff meeting lacerated Mr Ashoka, and the fact that Zenobia was a woman prevented the wound from healing. It left him restless and angry, dislocating his confident mastery of the day-to-day administration of his school. Mrs Kana found him subject to forgetfulness and moments of deep melancholia. He was brooding over Zenobia, how to discipline her, how to punish her. She had reduced his dignity in the presence of the entire staff, who were now probably waiting for his response. In fact, all the teachers and the principals in Lenasia might now have heard of Zenobia's challenge to his authority and be waiting to see what he would do. Could he ever hold another meeting with teachers in the staff-room without having re-established his dignity?

One afternoon the idea came to him: he would speak to Dr Whitecross about getting Zenobia transferred to another school. He felt so certain that the inspector would help him that he jumped from his chair and laughed. He telephoned Dr Whitecross and told him that he wished to speak to him privately on a very urgent matter.

'I shall be in my office until 4 pm,' Dr Whitecross said.

'Thank you, sir,' Mr Ashoka answered.

Mr Ashoka drove in his car to downtown Johannesburg. He parked in the street and then hurried to the inspector's office which was on the third floor of a new building that had already started to take on a dull bureaucratic appearance. As he emerged from the lift and passed by a small glass-panelled office — he failed to notice the word 'Enquiries', which had been drawn on cardboard with a red crayon — a sentry's voice cried out, 'Come back!' Mr Ashoka stopped and looked at a small ugly man who stood near the door of the office and beckoned him.

'What do you want?' the man asked.

'I have an appointment with Dr Whitecross.'

'They why didn't you tell me?'

Mr Ashoka did not answer for a moment, feeling humiliated, and then said, 'I am sorry. I didn't know.'

'Go then,' the man said, entering his cage-like office and sitting down.

Dr Whitecross welcomed Mr Ashoka in his rather spartan office — there was a large table with several chairs, a cabinet and nothing else.

'Now tell me, what is the problem?' Dr Whitecross said. 'I am sure I can help.'

Mr Ashoka told him what Zenobia had said at the meeting and ended by saying, 'You will appreciate that what she said was not only a challenge to me personally, but to the entire Department.'

'Of course, of course,' Dr Whitecross agreed readily.

45

'This is a very serious matter. But I don't think we should act hastily. You know the old saying about giving people enough rope. Let us see what she does next.'

'But, sir, my dignity?'

'You are a little too sensitive. There are always problems. I was a principal for many years and I know. Look at it in this way. If I make a report of the incident to the Department they will reject it. They will say she merely made a comment which cannot be regarded as insubordination. I suggest that you make an entry in the log book about what she said and I will record that you reported the matter to me.'

'Yes,' Mr Ashoka said, disappointed that the inspector had not decided on anything positive to discipline Zenobia.

'By the way, Mr Ashoka,' Dr Whitecross said, 'I have visited some primary schools in Lenasia and instructed the principals to implement the grouping system I spoke of. If your Teachers' Association receives any complaints you will know how to handle them.'

'Leave that to me,' Mr Ashoka assured him. 'But I will perhaps need your help in another matter. I have demoted some pupils from the matriculation class as I think that they are unfit to take their examination this year. Some disgruntled parents may soon complain to the Parents' Committee and they may come to see you.'

'That's a small matter,' Dr Whitecross answered. 'You are in complete charge of your school and after all you are doing what is best for the Indian child, just as I am doing my best for them. By the way my wife cannot stop speaking about the dinner . . . .'

'You must come and visit us again.'

'I will. But in the meantime can you write an article for

me on Hindu philosophy and the caste system. I am very interested in the Indian way of life.'

'Yes, certainly.'

'Please post it to me as soon as you have completed it.'

When Mr Ashoka left he felt that the inspector was probably right about giving people enough rope. There was practical wisdom in that. He would swallow his dignity and await his opportunity. In the meantime he would give Zenobia the impression that he was afraid of her. Soon she would overreach herself and be caught in the web of insubordination.

'I must give her enough rope . . .' he said, chuckling to himself as he got into his car and started it.

Before driving back home, Mr Ashoka went to the Planet Hotel in Fordsburg and had a few drinks.

After a few days, during the evening, three primary school teachers came to speak to Mr Ashoka about the new system of grouping pupils.

When the visitors entered the lounge Deva recognised one of them as his former teacher. He went up to him, shook his hand and sat down beside him on the settee.

Another of the teachers, a small, withered, dark man dressed in a maroon suit, set out their complaints and came to the point. 'In our opinion the entire system is psychologically damaging to children and can have serious social consequences in their lives. Mr Ashoka, as president of the Teachers' Association, can you do anything?'

Mr Ashoka thought for a while and then said, 'I don't think that the Teachers' Association can interfere in the administration of schools. This is an internal matter, the principals know best . . . .'

'It is not a question of interference. Surely the Teachers'

Association can give its opinion.'

Mr Ashoka smiled sardonically at the teacher and said, 'You know, frankly speaking, as an educationist and as a principal of a high school, I think that it is not a bad system at all. Every great educational authority from Rousseau to Nunn has laid emphasis on individual differences in children and has recommended that these should be taken into account in the educative process. Dr Whitecross has not sucked anything out of his thumb. This system is based on sound educational principles. Now the brighter children will be isolated early in life — nothing psychologically damaging about that — and they can progress without being unfairly held back by the dull ones. And the dull ones will have the advantage of receiving special attention . . . .'

'Like me,' Deva said, 'I always get special attention.'

'Don't take notice of him,' Mr Ashoka said, glaring at Deva for a moment. 'Gentlemen, I think you are ignorant of the theory and practice of modern education and that your objection is misguided. The Teachers' Association would look foolish if it protested against what is to the benefit of the Indian child and opposed a distinguished educationist such as Dr Whitecross who is an authority on Indian education.'

The teachers, dismayed at the lack of understanding shown by their president, rose to go. Suddenly Deva clapped his hands and shouted, 'I am president of the Clever Boys' Association!' and ran out of the room.

CHAPTER EIGHT

A meeting of the executive committee of the Teachers' Association was soon called by the secretary. The executive committee consisted of the president, the secretary, the treasurer and two representatives from each school, elected by teachers. When Zenobia was elected, Mr Ashoka was shocked. It had not occurred to him that the teachers would elect her after her challenge to his authority. He interpreted her election as an act of treachery, when in actual fact she had been elected because of the belief among teachers that she would be able to represent them most effectively. Mr Ashoka bitterly regretted not having been vigilant enough. He could easily have prevented her election by using the Disciplinary Committee. In fact he could have had the teachers vote for a candidate of his own choice. Now he would find himself opposed by her and he would not be able to silence her in the way he could at school.

The meeting of the Teachers' Association was held in its

premises on the second floor of a large building. Mr Ashoka, after winning the presidency the previous year, had had a large boardroom-type table installed at considerable expense to the Association. The table, he had felt, was necessary to project the status and importance of his position. But whereas then he had felt proud and happy, now he felt uneasy and insecure, because of Zenobia's election. Then there was another matter that troubled him. When he had been elected president he had been a vice-principal, a position that involved no direct relationship with the Department. Then, he could allow the Association to take up issues which now, as an officer of the Department, he would find embarrassing.

In fact, very soon after Mr Ashoka had declared the meeting open, a matter which promised to bring the Association into conflict with the Department came up for discussion. A certain teacher had been dismissed soon after graduating and receiving a post at a school. No reason had been given for his dismissal and the Association was asked to take legal action. After some discussion, Mr Ashoka said, 'Ladies and Gentlemen, the Director has the power in terms of the Education Act to dismiss a teacher at any time without offering a reason, and therefore I am afraid there is no legal redress.'

'I should like to disagree,' Zenobia said. 'I don't think this Association should accept injustice, however "legal" it may be. We must go to court in order to expose it publicly. If we don't do anything then any one of us can suffer the same fate.'

Zenobia's view gained support and Mr Ashoka began to panic. He could not allow the Association to take the Department to court.

'Ladies and gentlemen,' he pleaded, 'let us not be hasty in the matter. Let us take it up with the Director first. I am sure he will reconsider.'

He marshalled every argument he could against legal action, from his own influence with the Director, to the serious consequences that could befall a teacher who antagonised the government. When eventually the matter was put to the vote his view prevailed by a small majority.

The next matter that came up for discussion was an offer made in a letter from the African Teachers' Association 'to join hands in the struggle against discrimination.'

Mr Ashoka found himself in a difficult position again. He would be going against governmental edicts if he allowed his Association to work together with the African teachers. Dr Whitecross would not waste any time, when he came to hear of it, in telling him that he was committing treachery.

His fear generated this advice to the meeting: 'May I, as your President, make this plea? Instead of holding a joint meeting prematurely, let me meet the officials of the African Teachers' Association informally so that I can acquaint myself fully with the problems that are peculiar to them. Subsequently, after my report, we can decide on further communication. I am sure that this will be a better approach. Rushing into a joint meeting now may not be of any benefit in the long run.'

A few members seemed to accept the President's advice, but again Zenobia disagreed. 'I am sure that everyone present is aware of the ideology that shapes education in this country. Can the President go to the African teachers and ask them what problems are afflicting them? Aren't we aware of the inequalities?'

Mr Ashoka found himself checkmated and the teachers voted that a joint meeting should be arranged. Mr Ashoka consoled himself with the thought that he need not attend the meeting when it was called. Later, he could make the excuse that he had been taken ill.

Finally the issue of grouping pupils in the primary schools in accordance with the inspector's idea came up for discussion. The entire system was roundly condemned by everyone and Mr Ashoka remained silent. He realised that if he spoke of the merits of the system he could find himself accused of trying to defend Dr Whitecross. A strong resolution was taken against the system and Mr Ashoka had no option but to give his support.

The final item on the agenda was the election of the editor of the *Teachers' Chronicle* — the Association's news-letter. To Mr Ashoka's dismay, Zenobia was elected.

When the meeting ended it was dusk. Mr Ashoka went home, ate his supper silently and then locked himself in his study. He sat down at his table. He saw clearly that a time was coming when he would have to make a difficult choice: he would either have to take his stand with the Department or with the teachers. If he stood with the Department he would lose the support of teachers and find himself ousted as president of the Teachers' Association, and if he stood with the teachers the Department would be offended. And how was he now to face Dr Whitecross when he had promised him the Association's support? He looked at the rows of books on the shelves before him. He stood up, went to the sacred corner where the figure of Krishna stood, lit the wick in the clay bowl, joined the palms of his hands and bowed his head. But he did not know what to supplicate the god for. The dilemma facing him seemed to leave his mind in a limbo. He felt that perdition was about to overwhelm him for coming to the god with a mind emptied of thought, when he was saved by a knock on the door. Thankfully he turned away from the god and opened the door to Deva.

'I have been placed in the D class, dad,' Deva said, taking a pencil from his father's table and throwing it up and catching it like a juggler.

'Who put you in the D class?' Mr Ashoka asked angrily.

'You know, it was that inspector's clever idea, dad.'

Mr Ashoka took a step towards his son who had stopped playing with the pencil for a moment, and put his hand on his shoulder. 'It is all my fault,' he said penitently.

'Your fault, dad?'

'Yes, yes,' the father said, looking at his son tenderly. 'Go now to your mother and tell her to put you to bed. I am sure you don't have any homework.'

'No, dad,' Deva said, taking the pencil with him and continuing his juggling.

Mr Ashoka remained in his study for a long while, watching the burning wick in the clay bowl illuminating the face of Krishna.

The next day Mr Ashoka decided to use his presidential authority in preventing the secretary of the Teachers' Association from informing Dr Whitecross of the decision taken on his system of dividing the pupils.

'But you were in favour of the resolution,' the secretary said.

'There is a new development,' Mr Ashoka answered. 'I

have just spoken to the inspector and he is reconsidering the whole matter. There is every possibility that the system will be discontinued.'

CHAPTER NINE

The time arrived for the celebration of the Republic's tenth anniversary. The Department sent out circulars to all schools spelling out the details of the ceremony to be observed on the anniversary day. The headmaster would hold an assembly at eleven o'clock in the morning. He would read out to the pupils and teachers an address from the Director of Education. Thereafter the national flag would be raised and everyone would sing the national anthem. That would conclude the ceremony. Commemorative medals would be given to pupils and the school would close for the day. But the Department, remembering the trouble experienced at some schools during the celebration of the fifth anniversary, added a confidential supplement to the circular, stating that if principals felt that 'the holding of the celebrations would lead to any action or actions that may be deemed or construed to bring indignity to the national flag,' the celebrations should not be held and 'the school day should continue in the normal way.'

Mr Ashoka was determined that his school would participate in the celebrations: not only would he hold the prescribed ceremony in the morning, but he would ask the sportsmaster to arrange an athletics meeting for the afternoon. The fact that his predecessor had refused to celebrate the fifth anniversary was irrelevant to him. His duty was to obey.

Mr Ashoka — he now wore his academic gown daily — summoned a staff meeting and read the Department's circular to the teachers. He did not read the supplement to them as it did not concern them.

When he had finished, Zenobia raised an objection. 'I think it is clear to all of us that the voteless people of this country have no reason to celebrate.'

'I have decided in my capacity as principal that the celebrations will be held, just as my predecessor decided that the fifth anniversary celebrations should not be held and no one objected.'

The senior history teacher Mr Magan said that he supported Zenobia's view.

'That's very curious,' Mr Ashoka answered him. 'You go on teaching the Department's version of history as given in its text books and now you object to the celebration of an event in that history.'

The history teacher remained silent.

'Also,' Mr Ashoka continued, 'I want this school to hold an athletics meeting to mark the anniversary day. The sportsmaster will arrange this.'

'Yes, sir,' the sportsmaster agreed readily.

'And let me remind you,' Mr Ashoka said with emphasis, 'that all disciplinary problems will be handled by the

Disciplinary Committee.'

Beginning to feel confident that the majority of his staff supported him, Mr Ashoka turned to Zenobia. 'You have been,' he said, 'a sower of dissension since you arrived at the school this year. You can't expect everyone to think as you do. If you have an obsession to oppose everything I do at this school, then why don't you go to another school?'

Zenobia looked calmly at Mr Ashoka for a moment, then said, 'You have succumbed to herrenvolk authoritarianism. I shall not be forced to celebrate, do what you want to.'

'I shall instruct you!' Mr Ashoka threatened.

'Please yourself,' Zenobia said, waving her hand slightly so that her bangles chimed.

'The meeting is closed,' Mr Ashoka said, taking his file and marching out of the room, followed dutifully by Mr Saeed.

On the morning of Republic Day Mr Ashoka circulated the following notice to his staff: 'You are hereby instructed to come with your class pupils to the place of assembly at 11.00 am. Please maintain order and strict discipline.'

While the secretary took the notice around to all teachers, Mr Ashoka personally supervised the removal of the flag pole from its steel socket which was riveted to a cement platform. He then looped the flag rope around the pulley and watched while the pole was replaced in its socket.

The flag itself waited in its special case, locked safely in the strong-room. He would take it with him to assembly when the time came.

He now ordered Mr Saeed to summon the members of the Disciplinary Committee to his office. They came dutifully and he addressed them: 'Gentlemen, I have called you here because I have full confidence in your loyalty to the school. I fully appreciate the work you are doing and have inserted in each of your files commendatory reports on your sterling performances. As you know today is Republic Day. Orders are given for its celebration and as civil servants we must carry them out. I want your full co-operation if trouble occurs. As you know a few teachers are planning not to attend the ceremony and I strongly suspect that they have instigated some pupils to stay away. If teachers do not come to the assembly, I want you to leave them alone. The Department will handle them when the time is ripe. Insubordination will never go unpunished. But if pupils stay away I want you to go into the class-rooms, exercise your authority immediately, and bring them to the assembly place at once. Can I rely on you?'

'Yes, sir,' they all assented.

'And I want you to lead the singing of the national anthem. Mr Saeed has roneoed sufficient copies of the anthem for all pupils. Please hand these out now.'

Mr Saeed gave them the copies and they left the office.

When it was nearly eleven o'clock, Mr Ashoka opened the strong-room and from the safe took out the case containing the national flag. He closed the strong-room and, entering his secretary's office, asked her to give him the file containing the Director's speech. He then went outside where Mr Saeed joined him. Mr Ashoka expected to see the pupils emerging from their classrooms and marching to the assembly place, but he saw no one. Perhaps they had gone already. Striding towards the nearest classroom he received a shock when he looked through the window. All the pupils were still inside. He hurried to the next room, and the next (with Mr Saeed trying to keep up with him). Why had the pupils not gone to the assembly place? Had they not been told by the teachers? Or did Zenobia and her followers have such a hold on the minds of the pupils as to make them defy an order from him? They must have played on their emotions or threatened to fail them in their examinations. He turned to Mr Saeed and told him to summon the Disciplinary Committee immediately, and bring all the canes he could find in the office.

Soon the mathematics and science teachers joined their superior and Mr Saeed came with the canes.

'Gentlemen,' Mr Ashoka said, 'I want you to use the canes and get the pupils to the assembly place. But leave the senior pupils alone. I shall deal with them afterwards. Mr Saeed will lead you.'

Mr Saeed and the teachers went towards a room of junior pupils and entered. 'Boys and girls,' Mr Saeed said sternly, disregarding the presence of the geography teacher, 'I want you to go for assembly now.'

The pupils looked at the men with canes in bewilderment. Then, without warning, Mr Saeed went towards a pupil and lashed him on the left arm with the cane. The other teachers, regarding Mr Saeed's action as an order to attack, immediately set about belabouring the pupils, shouting 'Out! Out!' The terrified pupils rushed towards the door and went hurriedly to the assembly place.

'What are you doing?' the geography teacher protested, but neither Mr Saeed nor the other teachers paid any attention to him.

Soon the room was empty. Mr Saeed and the Disciplinary Committee then entered the room next door and enacted the same violent scene.

Mr Ashoka sternly watched the pupils rushing out of the rooms. As soon as Mr Saeed and the Disciplinary Committee had completed their task they reported to the principal.

'Thank you very much, gentlemen,' Mr Ashoka said. 'We shall now go on with the ceremony. Will one of you please take all the canes back to the office.'

When Mr Ashoka arrived at the assembly place, he saw that only a third of the school was present. And the only teachers present were the members of the Disciplinary Committee. He felt humiliated and bitter, his authority diminished. He had planned to raise the flag himself, but he would now ask Mr Saeed to do so. He hoped that Dr Whitecross would never come to hear of the defiance by pupils and teachers of his authority; it could lead the Department to doubt his competence and close his way to further promotion. He began the ceremony in a subdued voice.

'Members of the staff, boys and girls, today we are gathered here to commemorate the tenth anniversary of the Republic of South Africa. I want to read to you, on this important day in the life of the people of this country, the address of the Director of Education: "On this day our great nation renews its solemn pledge . . . ." '

When he had finished, he referred them to the roneoed copies of the national anthem which the Disciplinary Committee had distributed. He led them in the singing and when he looked up after the last line — 'We shall die for you South Africa' — he saw, standing at the rear away from everyone else, a figure in a grey suit — Dr Whitecross.

Mr Ashoka then asked Mr Saeed to raise the flag. Mr Saeed

tied the flag to the rope and pulled. The flag rose but halfway up the pulley jammed. Mr Ashoka looked apprehensively at Dr Whitecross and saw a taut solemn face looking at him. Mr Saeed tugged at the tope. After a while the pulley mechanism adjusted itself and the flag rose skywards.

Mr Ashoka ended the ceremony by dismissing the pupils and teachers, and after telling Mr Saeed to take care of the flag and the rope, hastened to where Dr Whitecross was standing. He extended his hand in greeting even before he reached him.

'Thank you for coming. My best wishes on your . . . our national day.'

'Can we go to your office?'

As they went towards the office they saw a group of teachers who had not attended the ceremony standing outside the staffroom. Dr Whitecross had seen them earlier when he had arrived, but had passed by without saying anything to them. Now, two of the teachers, seeing the principal and the inspector approach, slunk away.

When Dr Whitecross reached the teachers he stopped. 'Ladies and gentlemen,' he said, 'you were not at the ceremony.'

'No,' Zenobia answered.

Dr Whitecross turned to Mr Ashoka.

'I want a statement from them that they did not attend . . . in triplicate.' His voice was grave and there was a tone of suppressed anger.

The two men then walked on towards the office.

In the office Dr Whitecross asked, 'Did you instruct all your teachers to attend the flag-raising ceremony?'

'Yes, sir,' Mr Ashoka said, hurriedly producing the

notice.

'Now, what are you going to do with the pupils and teachers who refused to attend?'

'I shall ask them to remain. Lessons must continue.'

Mr Ashoka hurriedly wrote a notice to that effect, went into his secretary's office and handed it to her to take around. Then he returned.

'The situation is very serious,' Dr Whitecross said. 'The teachers who were absent from the ceremony have insulted the State. The Department will require a full report of what happened today. I also want you to submit a list of the names of all teachers and pupils who did not attend the ceremony.'

'I shall do that, sir.'

'I shall come tomorrow for your report and the statement of the teachers who were not present.'

The inspector rose to go. Mr Ashoka accompanied him to his car. But instead of standing for a while and saying a few words as he usually did, the inspector got into his car and drove away.

Mr Ashoka returned to his office and brooded. If he stated in his report that the majority of the teachers were absent from the ceremony the Department could decide to institute an official enquiry. If he did not, Dr Whitecross had observed the number of teachers present and he could accuse him of distorting the facts. Perhaps if he accused the English teachers of intimidating pupils and teachers . . . . He decided to take Mr Saeed into his confidence so that should there be an enquiry their evidence would coincide. He went to Mr Saeed's office. It meant breaking protocol, as a senior did not go to a junior's office, but he needed his support now.

'I don't think,' he said, 'that the pupils and teachers who stayed away from the ceremony did so of their own free will. I think they were intimidated by the English teachers. What is your opinion?'

'I think you are right, Mr Ashoka. Let us see now how they will bear the brunt.'

'Thank you, Mr Saeed. I value your judgement. Please inform the English teachers that the inspector will come tomorrow for their statement.'

For the first time Mr Ashoka felt that his deputy, a man of few words, was of some substance. He had never thought much of him before and had wondered how he had acquired his B.A. degree. The man's entire bearing and temperament was that of a servant, and a very servile one. If he had a mind of his own, he had never revealed it until this day. In his distress Mr Ashoka was thankful for his deputy's support and thought a little better of him.

When he returned to his office, he thought that his strategy to isolate the English teachers was an astute one. They would not dare to complain that there were other teachers who had stayed away: their image of principled opposition would crumble. They now faced a crucial test. They had to put down their opposition in writing, which was something different from the luxury of glib talking.

He began writing his report and it was late in the afternoon after everyone had gone home that he ended it with the following paragraph: 'I wish to make the following unequivocal accusation. The English teachers were fully responsible for instigating some pupils and teachers not to attend the Republic Day celebration ceremony. They have been abusing their function as teachers by using the Department's time to indoctrinate pupils politically. They have been guilty of consistently flouting my instructions and their behaviour is beginning to have an adverse effect on the tone of the school. Many parents have complained to me that their children's time is being wasted by these teachers who are engaged in furthering their political grievances through innocent children. I shall be pleased at whatever action the Department may deem fit to take in the circumstances.'

The next day when Dr Whitecross came to the school Mr Ashoka said to him: 'The English teachers were responsible for what happened yesterday. Here is my report.'

Dr Whitecross took the report and put it into his bag. 'I want their statement,' he said. 'Have they given it to you?'

'No. Perhaps they have refused to write it.'

'Then ask them to come here immediately.'

Mr Ashoka went over to his secretary and asked her to summon the offenders. When the six teachers entered the office, Dr Whitecross said sternly, 'Can I have your statement, please.'

Zenobia opened her handbag and gave him a letter which he opened and read: 'We, the undersigned, were not present at the ceremony commemorating Republic Day.'

'This is not a statement,' Dr Whitecross snapped.

'If you had something else in mind then you should have said so,' Zenobia replied.

'I want a statement of your reasons for not attending the ceremony,' Dr Whitecross said, a little angrily.

'You didn't ask for that,' Zenobia reminded him.

'I want that statement now.'

'We are not obliged to give it.'

'If you don't, someone else will come for it.'

'The police?'

'No,' Dr Whitecross said defensively. 'Someone from the Department.'

'I am afraid we will have nothing further to say.'

Dr Whitecross winced. No teacher had ever spoken to him in that forthright manner. 'I am here to help you,' he said, in a sudden transition of tone, 'should the Department decide to take drastic action against you. I am not your enemy, but your friend.'

For a moment the teachers were suprised by the inspector's changed attitude. 'We do not need any friends in this issue,' Zenobia said wryly. 'In that case,' the inspector said, addressing Mr Ashoka, 'we shall leave the matter in the hands of the Department.'

When the teachers had left, Mrs Kana came in with tea.

'There are always problems,' Dr Whitecross said, sipping his tea. 'But what can we do? We have to handle them as best we can.'

'What action do you think the Department will take?' Mr Ashoka asked.

'None.'

'None?'

'There are political considerations. The Department will not want to make martyrs of them.'

'Of course not.'

Dr Whitecross did not tell Mr Ashoka that he had no intention of submitting his report to the Department. He did not want to give the Director of Education the impression that he could not handle problematical situations at schools under his control. In fact the report might not only lead to further complications, but also impede his way up the 'promotion ladder'. Dr Whitecross's present ambition extended to the Deputy Director's post; his ultimate goal was the Directorship.

'But the Department never forgets,' Dr Whitecross went on. 'It always believes in giving trouble makers enough rope.'

'Your image is very appropriate.' Mr Ashoka began to feel that the strain that had entered into his relationship with Dr Whitecross the previous day was beginning to ease. Basically his superior was a genial man, and he would always have the highest respect for him.

'I have to go now,' Dr Whitecross said, rising from his chair. 'If you have any further problems, please let me know.'

Mr Ashoka accompanied the inspector to his car and shut the door for him. Returning to his office, he remembered the supplementary confidential report to principals on raising the flag. Why had the inspector not referred to it? Would the Department contemplate acting against him for not having exercised his judgement in a responsible manner, especially as it was prevented by political considerations from acting against the rebellious teachers? Suddenly, his anxieties had returned.

Unknown to Mr Ashoka, as the inspector drove away in his car, there was a parcel covered in gift wrapping on the back seat. In it there was an expensive shirt and tie, and a very expensive tie pin and cuff link set, with a ribboned card stating: Best Wishes for Republic Day — A.M. Saeed.

Also unknown to Mr Ashoka was Mr Saeed's meteoric rise up the 'promotion ladder', thanks to the influence of a wealthy relative over persons in the upper hierarchy of the Department. He had achieved the post of deputy principal after teaching for five years instead of the usual ten.

Mr Ashoka had waited for fifteen years to achieve the post; others never did, remaining ordinary teachers till retirement day.

CHAPTER TEN

It troubled Mr Ashoka that only the mathematics and science teachers had attended the flag-raising ceremony. Did Zenobia and her clique exercise control over the minds of teachers? What did they say to them? Did they hold political seminars and indoctrinate them? Or were they, by means of jeering cynical remarks about him, subtly influencing the teachers and pupils to turn against him and defy authority? He had to know what they were saying in order to counter their intrigue against him.

After a few days he came up with the idea of an inter-communication system which would allow him to hear whatever they said and so forestall any conspiracies they might hatch against him. But how was he to obtain such a system? He could not use the school funds for the purpose as the Department did not allow principals such luxuries. In any case there was not enough money in the bank. Only the Parents' Committee could obtain the money. He decided to summon them to a meeting.

'Gentlemen,' Mr Ashoka addressed them, 'it will be appreciated by you that there is a communication problem at school. If I want to communicate with a teacher I have to send my secretary or the vice-principal to call him, or if a teacher wants to communicate with me he has to come himself or send a pupil with a message. Then again if I wish to communicate with all the pupils I have to hold a special assembly and if I wish to communicate with all the teachers I have to hold a staff meeting. You will agree that valuable time is being wasted. What we need is an intercommunication system.'

'There is a problem here,' Dr Raj said. 'Even assuming we had the money to pay for such a system many parents might feel that we could spend it on more useful educational equipment that would benefit the pupils.'

'What could be more useful to pupils,' Mr Ashoka countered, 'than time saved? In the educational process time is of the utmost importance. It was the great Dante who said, "He who grieves most grieves for wasted time." ' (Mr Ashoka had never read Dante. He had seen the epigram in a magazine.) 'Besides time saved, the system will enable me to exercise better discipline over the pupils and teachers. I could listen in to lessons and make helpful comments.'

'It may be very useful,' the doctor agreed, 'but there is the practical problem of raising the money. Mr Ashoka, you will agree that raising three to four thousand rands isn't going to be easy.'

'I understand,' Mr Ashoka replied. 'But you have willingly accepted serving on this committee under the stipulated conditions. Your duty is to do everything possible for the betterment of the education of our children. You cannot escape your responsibilities. Gentlemen, you have a proposal before you to accept or reject.'

Mr Ismail, the treasurer, now spoke and said that the Committee should work in harmony with the principal. He felt sure that they could gather the money. He was prepared to donate a lounge suite from his furniture store and if the other members made similar contributions a raffle could be organised and the money collected.

'That is something positive,' Mr Ashoka said in commendation.

The doctor spoke again and said that he still held to his earlier view that many parents might not agree about the usefulness of the intercommunication system above other equipment, but if the matter was put to the vote and the majority agreed to collect the money and purchase the system he would go along with the idea.

The matter was put to the vote and four out of the seven members were in favour of the motion.

Thereafter the Committee devoted itself to planning money-raising methods. The raffle idea was discussed again and when two other members offered to contribute an encyclopaedia and a hi-fi set, the idea was accepted. Mr Ashoka agreed to give raffle tickets to pupils and teachers at school to help in the effort.

Then Dr Raj raised a matter in the most delicate way possible. He said that various parents had complained to the Committee about the demotion of their children from the standard ten class and that there seemed to be much dissatisfaction. He was sensible that Mr Ashoka had acted in the best interests of the pupils. He would be happy if the principal would explain to the Committee the reasons for the demotions, so that they could inform the parents.

'Gentlemen,' Mr Ashoka answered, 'the decision to

demote the pupils was taken in consultation with my teachers. They felt that my predecessor had been rather lax in promotions and that it would be in the best interests of the pupils to spend another year in the standard nine class. That is all there is to it.'

The Committee did not find the explanation convincing, but did not say so. Neither did they tell Mr Ashoka that many parents were beginning to have doubts about his competence in administering the school — they had all heard about what happened on Republic Day. Many of them had been angered by the change in school uniforms, for it involved them in needless expense — some had said they would not purchase new uniforms until their children had worn out the old ones. The new name of the school had occasioned as much amusement as anger and many considered it a ruse by the principal to perpetuate his own name.

The sale of raffle tickets did not go smoothly at school, although all the teachers and pupils were issued with tickets to sell. Many teachers realised that the intercommunication system would be used by the principal to listen secretly to lessons and even to private conversations, and discouraged the pupils from selling tickets. But Mr Ashoka countered their action by using the Disciplinary Committee to sell the tickets to the public. Soon the money was collected by the Parents' Committee and the intercommunication system was purchased.

When the electrician came to install the system Mr Ashoka said to him, 'I want this sytem to operate one way only; that is, I should be able to communicate with pupils and teachers in the various classrooms but they should not be able to communicate with me. I don't want them to listen in to any private conversation going on in this office.'

'That can be done quite easily,' the electrician said, not quite knowing why anyone should wish to purchase an expensive intercommunication system and then reduce its effectiveness by half.

Soon Mr Ashoka was seated in his office beside a microphone and a control panel of switches with flickering green and red lights.

CHAPTER ELEVEN

One day when Mr Ashoka came home after school he saw a police car parked outside his front gate. His wife, looking very grave, met him at the door.

In the lounge, sitting near Deva, was a police officer: a bulbous, chocolate-dark man with curly hair and a thin moustache.

'What is the problem?' Mr Ashoka asked, looking at Deva.

'You will have to take greater care of your son,' the officer said, smiling affably and opening a file that was in his hand.

'No boy could have a better father,' Mr Ashoka said with emphasis.

'Have you heard that, Deva?' the officer asked, placing his hand paternally on Deva's shoulder. 'See what you have done today . . . brought disgrace to your good parents.'

'Disgrace?' Mr Ashoka said, a little impatiently. 'What have you done?'

'I am sorry to inform you,' the officer told Mr Ashoka, 'that your son, together with two other boys, was caught shop-lifting at the supermarket . . . . '

'Shop-lifting? When?'

'Today . . . . '

'Why were you not at school?' Mr Ashoka asked Deva angrily.

Deva looked at his father with his large liquid eyes.

'First, sir, let me give you the facts,' the officer said. 'At 11.20 am the owner of the supermarket, Mr Khan, came to the police station to lodge the complaint that three boys from Alpha Primary School had been caught trying to leave the supermarket without paying for the following items in their possession: two bars of chocolates, 250 grams each; two packets of Three Rings biscuits, 200 grams each; 450 grams of walnuts, and one bottle of Bouquet perfume. I went immediately to the supermarket and found them with the items still in their hands.'

'What are you going to do?' Mr Ashoka asked in a troubled voice.

'Nothing,' the officer said. 'I know you can look after your son. I don't want to take him in front of a magistrate. And fortunately for him Mr Khan, at my request, has decided to withdraw the charge against him and his two friends.'

'Thank you very much,' Mr Ashoka said, feeling relieved.

Mrs Ashoka immediately went to the kitchen to get a fruit drink for the officer.

While having his drink, the officer said to Deva, 'Son, you should be thankful that you have such a wonderful father.'

Deva looked at his father with an amused smile.

'Obey him always and be good,' the officer said, finishing his drink and rising to go.

Mr Ashoka shook the officer's hand and asked him his name. 'I am senior officer Ayer,' he answered with a felicitous smile. Mr Ashoka accompanied him to his car, smiling and talking to him as though he were a friend of long standing. He did not want to give any of his neighbours who might be watching the impression that the officer's arrival with Deva spelt trouble.

As soon as Mr Ashoka re-entered his house he demanded that Deva tell him the entire story.

'The policeman told everything,' Deva said.

'No, tell me again.'

'I am not going to,' Deva answered, impishly rather than defiantly.

'So you are a thief now,' his father shouted. 'You have disgraced us, you idiot!'

Mrs Ashoka stood in the kitchen doorway, looking miserable.

'You ran away from school,' the father went on, 'that's one crime. Then you went to steal, that's another.'

'I didn't steal,' Deva answered, 'I didn't have any money so I took the things.'

'That's the same as stealing,' his father reminded him.

'It isn't,' Deva said. 'Those who have money and take things are stealing.'

Mr Ashoka was in no mood to enter into a debate with his son on his novel definition of theft and demanded to know why he had run away from school.

'I didn't go to school today,' Deva answered.

'Not at school!'

This realisation almost asphyxiated him as a constricting

pain gripped his chest. He hurried to the telephone and dialled the home number of Deva's principal. The telephone rang for a long while on the other end and then was lifted. A frail voice answered. But Mr Ashoka remained silent when it flashed across his mind that Deva's principal was ignorant of what had happened. If he had known he would by now have informed him. Officer Ayer's gracious decision not to do anything about the theft came to mind. If he now informed the principal everyone would come to know. He replaced the telephone on its cradle after listening to a frantic repetition of 'hullos'. He turned around to tell Deva that he was fortunate that his principal was not at home.

But Deva was gone. Mr Ashoka went to the kitchen, thinking he had followed his wife there. But he was not there. Husband and wife searched the house and then went outside. Deva had disappeared.

'I am sure the police officer can help us again,' Mrs Ashoka said to her husband as they re-entered the house. She sat down on the settee and began to cry into the end of her georgette sari.

'Perhaps he has gone to play,' her husband said, fearing that any attempt to search for Deva might bring the theft at the supermarket to the attention of his neighbours.

Mr Ashoka went to his study and sat down on his chair. Hatred for his son mushroomed within him. The boy had repaid him for all his fatherly care by running away. He remained there sphinx-like until his wife came to call him for supper.

Husband and wife ate in silence. Deva's absence weighed on them as though the very soul of the house had vanished. The hatred he had felt earlier gave way to natural affection.

Whatever his son had done did not matter. He wanted him back.

'Deva must come back home,' he said. 'Where can he go?'

A sob escaped from his wife's lips.

'He will come back as soon as he is hungry,' he comforted his wife.

After supper he went to his study again. He lit the sacred lamp and stood beside the image of Krishna and supplicated the god to bring his son home to him. Then he sat down in his chair.

After about ten minutes he heard a faint knock on the front door. He hurried to open it at the same time as his wife who came from the kitchen. The door opened to a smiling Deva.

Mr Ashoka, his pulse racing with happiness, did not ask Deva any questions.

Saying that he had some work to finish he returned to his study. There he immediately went to the brass deity and offered thanks.

Then he sat down at his table, took a blank exercise book and began to write. It was an impulsive act, perhaps a conditioned reflex acquired from his habit of keeping his log-book up to date at school. 'My dearest Deva' — he wrote — 'when you were absent at supper time I realised how much I loved you. However wrong your action may have been in taking the articles at the supermarket, I shall never blame you. I shall always cherish you as my dearest object in this world. I need not remind you that my whole life has been directed to your welfare and education and I shall continue doing so whatever happens in the future. I can never describe the joy I felt today when I heard your knock on the door and saw you when I opened it. Whatever agony there was in my heart — and in recent weeks there has been much — blew away. Do not ever go away again. The time you were away was so unbearably painful that I would not like to go through it again.'

Mr Ashoka retired to bed after midnight, but sleep did not come to him, through sheer happiness. His mind seemed to be a shrine enclosing the image of Deva. He rose and went to his bedroom and switching on the light looked at him sleeping peacefully. He kneeled down beside his bed and took his hand. Then very gently he caressed his forehead, pushing back his hair. The boy smiled faintly in his sleep. The father smiled in return.

CHAPTER TWELVE

There was much controversy among teachers and pupils about the intercommunication system at Ashoka High School. Again the English teachers were the most critical, charging Mr Ashoka with listening to them surreptitiously; interrupting lessons several times a day when he wished to say something or other; calling teachers and pupils to the office on the flimsiest of pretexts; and making unnecessary, trivial announcements. Teachers also discovered that the sytem operated one way only. Criticism reached him through his 'Gestapo', as the mathematics and science teachers were now being called by other teachers and pupils. When the accusation that he was beginning to behave like a 'paranoiac dictator' (a phrase that could have come only from Zenobia's lips) came to his ears he felt very bitter. His inability to take action against the English teachers still rankled within him.

Officer Ayer's arrival gave him an idea. He could tell the officer of the trouble he was experiencing from Zenobia and her supporters, who were nothing more than politicians in disguise, bent on creating turmoil at school. Officer Ayer could easily speak to his senior and then take action; perhaps get the government to place banning orders on them so that they would be permanently prevented from entering educational institutions.

Mr Ashoka went to the police station during the late evening as he did not want to be seen on his way there. The building was in a dusty part of Lenasia once known as Dry Bones, now called Greyville, with depressing regiments of block houses, disorderly front gardens, back-yards piled with junk and rusted remnants of motor-cars, and peach and plum and apricot trees looking drearily out of place.

When Mr Ashoka entered the charge office he saw a constable behind the counter and a tall bearded man in a turban and black cloak. The two men did not look at him. He stood nearby while the constable questioned the man and wrote along dotted lines on the inside of a file. Mr Ashoka learnt that the man had come to complain about a burglary.

'Did you give anyone permission to break into your house?' the constable asked.

The man looked at the constable in bewilderment, then said, 'What do you mean? How could I give anyone permission?'

'You have to answer the question when making a complaint.'

'Why must I answer a silly question?'

The constable, a young fellow, looked blankly at the complainant.

'It is the rule here,' he said, placing his pen nib on the

dotted line, and posing the question again.

'Listen,' the bearded man said, 'how can you ask me such a stupid question? Do I look stupid? Didn't you go to school?'

The thrust made no impression on the constable, who repeated, 'You have to answer the question. It is the rule.'

'What rule? Who made it?'

'At every police station . . . . '

'I don't care. I come to complain and you make rules about my complaint. If I gave anyone permission why should I come here? This is stupid!'

The man turned around, fuming.

'What do you think of this rule?' he said to Mr Ashoka.

'I don't know all the facts,' Mr Ashoka said noncommittally, 'but I think there are certain formalities . . . . '

'You have said it, sir,' the constable interjected thankfully. 'You know about law.'

'Can I speak to officer Ayer?' Mr Ashoka asked, not wishing to get involved in any further dispute. 'It is a matter of urgency.'

'Of course, sir,' the constable said, jumping down from his stool, very pleased to help his saviour. He led Mr Ashoka into a corridor, knocked at a door, and asked him to go in.

Officer Ayer stopped writing as soon as he saw the headmaster, and asked him to sit down opposite him. He folded his arms, and beamed. Mr Ashoka did not know how to begin and felt a little embarrassed. The officer continued beaming at him.

'I have a problem,' Mr Ashoka began hesitantly, 'which is not connected with Deva this time. I wonder if you can help me?'

'Tell me the problem and perhaps I can.'

'I need not remind you,' Mr Ashoka said in a confidential tone, 'that you are an officer of the law, that you demand good discipline from people. Now at school I am faced with the problem of several teachers behaving in a way that threatens law and order. They are always instigating others to rebel.'

'Have they broken the law?' the officer asked.

'No, but they are to all intents and purposes working against the law by bringing politics into school, disrupting school life and corrupting the children.'

'You have come to the wrong department,' officer Ayer said. 'You must go to Security. I only work on criminal cases.'

'And where can I find Security?'

The officer wrote the address in downtown Johannesburg on a sheet of paper.

'Who is the man I should speak to?' Mr Ashoka enquired, taking the note.

'Colonel van der Spuy.'

Mr Ashoka thanked the officer and took his leave. On his way out of the charge office the constable jumped off his stool — he was alone now — and accompanied Mr Ashoka to his car. 'If ever you have any problems, sir, I shall be ready to help.'

Mr Ashoka, the next afternoon, drove to Johannesburg and had no difficulty in finding Security headquarters. He parked his car nearby and entered the five-storey building. He saw a man with a tray of files waiting for the lift and he asked him where he could find the colonel.

'Fifth floor, Room 22,' the man answered as the lift

door opened. The man entered the lift, did not wait for Mr Ashoka to enter but pressed the door button. The doors closed and the lift ascended.

It occurred to Mr Ashoka that the lift was for whites only. He looked to see if there was a lift for non-whites hidden somewhere in a corner of the foyer, but there wasn't. He decided to climb the stairs. As he walked up his determination to have Zenobia and her supporters ousted from the teaching profession hardened. As soon as he had informed the Colonel about their activities, they would be called up for interrogation. In fact he would tell the colonel that they should be picked up at midnight and interrogated unremittingly till sunrise about their motives in resisting legitimate authority.

When he reached the top floor he was panting and he stood for a while in the corridor to regain his breath. Then he went towards Room 22 and knocked. A voice asked him to enter.

Colonel van der Spuy was seated at his desk. He was a huge man whose size made the office look small, as though designed for a dwarf.

Mr Ashoka stood respectfully before the colonel and gave his reasons for coming.

'I know everything about Zenobia,' the colonel said. 'She is a naughty woman, isn't she?'

The colonel's frivolous response unsettled Mr Ashoka, and his further remark positively frightened him.

'I know everything that is happening at your school.'

'Everything, sir?'

'Everything connected with security. Otherwise I would not keep my job.'

'Can anything be done to discipline them, sir?'

'We will take action when necessary. Don't worry head-master, we are watching everybody . . . . Thank you for coming.'

In Mr Ashoka's fearful eyes the colonel seemed to increase in girth until he looked like a giant squid that dangerously threatened to occupy the entire office space and crush him to death. He left quickly.

He walked down the stairs, keeping his hand on the railing. So Security had its eyes on the school? He was being watched as well as the others. What if the spies told lies about him? When he reached the foyer he began to panic and hurried out of the building as though he were pursued.

He drove to Fordsburg and stopped in front of the Planet Hotel.

CHAPTER THIRTEEN

Mr Ashoka sat down at a table in a corner of the bar and when the waiter came ordered whisky and soda. The liquor eased the tension within him. Well, he thought, if Security had their eyes on the school he had nothing to fear. He had always carried out his duties to the letter; Dr White-cross could attest to that. His enemies were the ones who had reason to be afraid. In fact, he would give them the opportunity to indulge in seditious rhetoric until the time came for Security to twist its thong around their necks.

The waiter brought another whisky and soda. Mr Ashoka looked at him in surprise: he had not ordered the drink. The waiter pointed to a man sitting four tables away from him and said, 'With the compliments of Prince Yusuf.'

Mr Ashoka looked at the man, who immediately rose from his chair with his drink in one hand and cigar in the other and came over to him.

'May I have the pleasure of meeting you,' he said, placing his drink on the table and extending his hand. He then sat down on a chair.

He was a well-built man with a face as elegant-looking in profile as it was from the front. Waves of dark russet hair flowed from his smooth dune-bronze forehead; his black eyes were recessed and impressively shaped. He was the most handsome man Mr Ashoka had ever seen in his life. He was enclosed in fashion's best: there was an expensive, hand-tailored, dark brown check suit; a beige shirt and matching tie decorated with rust-coloured proteas; an immaculate silk handkerchief peering from a coat pocket; gold cuff-links and a tie pin inset with amber gem stones; a large flashing gold ring; an expensive gleaming gold watch.

'I have seen you before in Lenasia,' Prince Yusuf said amicably, sipping liquor.

'I am a school principal.'

'Of course, I can see that. Which school?'

'Ashoka High. The school is named after me.'

'Wonderful! My cousin's children attend your school. I am originally from Durban where everyone called me Prince Yusuf. I recently moved into Lenasia because of business in this golden city.'

Mr Ashoka looked at the man in admiration. He was the darling of the gods and fortune. Besides his splendid appearance, he was so completely at ease with himself and the world, so sybaritic in the enjoyment of his liquor and cigar.

'I spend my evenings in Hillbrow. What do you do of an evening, Mr Ashoka?'

'I have my responsibilities.'

'Of course — you are an important man. But you must relax.'

'I study during evenings.'

'Yes, that's very good. But what I mean is, how do you enjoy yourself? Pass the time?'

Mr Ashoka could not answer.

'How do you amuse yourself?'

The man's insistent questioning left him feeling that he was missing a primrose principle of existence, and that his own life was one of inertia. Prince Yusuf, in his festive, epicurean disposition, seemed to present a dimension of living Mr Ashoka was unaware of.

'Perhaps you relax with whisky,' Prince Yusuf said laughingly, signalling to the waiter for more drinks.

'Tell me, Mr Ashoka, what car do you drive?'

'A Prefect.'

'Have you seen mine? Come with me to the door and you will see it.'

Prince Yusuf led Mr Ashoka to the glass door of the bar, and, pointing at a car in the street, said, 'That silver-grey one. Do you know what model it is?'

He could not say. To him a car was a means of transport from one place to another. Expensive limousines were the toys of the puerile rich, whom he had always considered as leading meaningless lives in contrast to his own purposeful existence, devoted to academic fulfilment.

'That's a Mustang,' Prince Yusuf informed Mr Ashoka. 'Do you know what a mustang is?'

'Yes . . . no,' he answered, feeling inadequate.

'It's a wild prairie horse. I bought the car when I was in America a few months ago.' Prince Yusuf led Mr Ashoka back to the table. 'I returned by plane and had my car shipped here.'

Mr Ashoka began to feel that an engrossment with

material things had its own peculiar charm. He looked at Prince Yusuf and felt drawn towards him.

'I will pick you up at home one evening and we will go to Hillbrow. That is the place for virile men. Lenasia is dead.'

'That's true,' Mr Ashoka agreed.

'You agree with me? That's very good.'

The waiter came with drinks. Prince Yusuf tipped him so liberally that Mr Ashoka was surprised.

Then a beggar entered the bar. He was an old man and though not in rags, his clothes needed washing. He wore a small red fez. While Mr Ashoka looked for some cents in his pocket, Prince Yusuf gave the man a two-rand note. Again Mr Ashoka was surprised.

'Don't you think you have given the beggar too much?'

'Not at all. He may have a family. One never knows what he may have gone through in life.'

'He may be a swindler.'

'It is better to think well of people,' Prince Yusuf answered, pouring soda into their glasses and putting in ice-cubes. 'After business, pleasure. That's my motto,' Prince Yusuf said, handing Mr Ashoka his glass.

As Mr Ashoka took his glass, clinked it with Prince Yusuf's and put it to his lips, he saw in the golden liquid the affluent aura of the man before him.

'Here, have a havana cigar,' Prince Yusuf said, taking two cigars out of his pocket and unwrapping them from cellophane covers. He gave one to Mr Ashoka and lit it for him, using a lighter with the look of an authentic piece of gold nugget.

'Sometimes Hillbrow can be dangerous,' Prince Yusuf said, lighting his own cigar and blowing a jet of smoke.

'But then that's life. There is no pleasure without some danger. And I always have my gun with me.'

'Gun?'

He produced a revolver from a concealed holster and put it on the table. 'It's a Beretta. Just hold it.'

Mr Ashoka looked fearfully around to see if anyone was looking. The sweep of his eyes took in an amorphous group of men sitting around a table at the far end of the room, drinking and conversing.

'You must not take it out here,' Mr Ashoka said apprehensively, pushing the gun away from him.

'Oh, don't be afraid,' Prince Yusuf said coolly. 'I have a permit for it.'

Mr Ashoka took a mouthful of liquor hurriedly. Instead of feeling relieved, a sudden constriction gripped his throat. The constriction was triggered by a feeling of insignificance: he was merely a frightened mouse, scuttling through corridors, hiding in corners, living on yellowed paper and wood-shavings, perversely nursing his ego and deluding himself that he was of some consequence.

'There are many envious people and I have to protect myself,' Prince Yusuf explained, putting the gun away. 'If ever you have any trouble from anyone, let me know. I shall stand by you.'

'Thank you very much,' Mr Ashoka said gratefully. 'You know, at my school there are several teachers who are always giving me problems.'

'Just tell me who they are and I will crush them even before they can spell "sir",' Prince Yusuf said laughingly.

Mr Ashoka extended his hand gratefully to Prince Yusuf. The teachers who were on his side at school, even Mr Saeed, supported him because they were duty-bound and feared the Department. Here was a man who stood beside him freely, a man with a gun.

Prince Yusuf signalled to the waiter who was standing in a corner and he brought more drinks.

Mr Ashoka remembered that Dr Raj had been difficult about the intercommunication system and, still feeling piqued about the objection he had raised, mentiond his name as one of his enemies.

'He must be a parasite, exploiting the sick and poor,' Prince Yusuf said. 'Don't waste your time. Here take this gun and go and blow his brains out.'

'No, no, please put the gun away.'

'Let's go in my Mustang now.'

'No, please, not now,' Mr Ashoka said in trepidation, placing a restraining hand on Prince Yusuf's arm. 'There is a time for everything. I value your friendship sincerely.'

'Then let's drink to our friendship,' Prince Yusuf said, smiling.

They clinked glasses.

'I have to go now,' Prince Yusuf said, looking at his watch. 'I have to meet Mr Ziegler, the interior decorator. I owe him some money which I want to pay him.'

He stood up, put his hand into his inner coat pockets and frowned. He then put his hand into his back trouser pocket and produced a thick wad of ten rand notes. Mr Ashoka had never seen anyone carry so much money in his pocket.

'I think I left my cheque book at home,' Prince Yusuf said, putting the cash back into his pocket.

'But you have enough money,' Mr Ashoka said.

'Not enough to pay an interior decorator. Do me a favour. Can you give me a cheque and I will return it to you as soon as I can.'

'Of course,' Mr Ashoka obliged. 'Take my cheque book and write out a page. How much do you need?'

'Not much,' Prince Yusuf said, using a pen that Mr Ashoka was convinced was twenty-two carat gold. 'Five hundred will do.'

'Go ahead,' Mr Ashoka urged him, feeling that lending Prince Yusuf five hundred rands was a small favour in return for his allegiance. After writing out the cheque and obtaining Mr Ashoka's signature, Prince Yusuf then noted the principal's address in his diary and was ready to leave.

The two men shook hands.

After Prince Yusuf had left, Mr Ashoka ordered whisky to celebrate his good fortune in meeting him. At last he had gained a potent ally in his struggle with his enemies. A genie had emerged from the golden fire of a whisky bottle to do his bidding.

When after a few days Prince Yusuf did not turn up to return Mr Ashoka's money, he did not feel upset. He rationalised that life never followed an even pattern. Prince Yusuf might have had an unexpected visitor, or his car might have broken down, or business might have taken him to New York.

CHAPTER FOURTEEN

At ten o'clock one morning Colonel van der Spuy entered Mr Ashoka's office.

'Sit down, please,' the principal said, recognising him. He rose from his chair and extended his hand. 'I am sure I can help you, sir.'

'Yes,' the colonel said. 'You have a teacher here by the name of Mrs Zenobia Hansa. I want to speak to her.'

'Yes certainly. I hope it's not in connection with any political matter, sir. You know we don't tolerate any politics here.'

'No, it's only a private matter.'

Mr Ashoka went into his secretary's office and asked her to call Zenobia. He did not return to his office but went outside and stood in the corridor, trying to control the trepidation that had erupted within him as soon as he recognised the colonel. Several questions assailed him now. Had the colonel come as a result of his complaint? Would he tell Zenobia of his accusation? What would the colonel say to him if he found her innocent? And why, in his first words to the colonel, had he implied that politics played no part in the life of his school — when he had gone to the colonel over politics? Would he perceive the contradiction? Would he not begin to suspect him?

Zenobia appeared before Mr Ashoka suddenly, like a magician's creation. His abstracted mind had not recorded her approach. 'You . . . have a visitor . . . in the office. He is waiting for you.'

Zenobia went towards the office and entered.

'Please close the door,' the colonel said. He had usurped Mr Ashoka's chair after closing the door leading to the secretary's office. He introduced himself and asked Zenobia to be seated opposite him.

Zenobia knew the names of several security officers because of their involvement in political trials. But she had not heard of Van der Spuy before.

'I am making an investigation,' he said, taking out his note-book and pen from his coat pocket. 'Tell me, do you know a man named Tela?'

'Yes. We taught at the same school last year.'

'The school in Fordsburg?'

'Yes.'

'Did you have any dealings with him?'

'What do you mean?'

'Well, did you communicate with him outside school?'

'What do you mean by that?'

'For instance, did he visit you at home?'

'Yes, he did. Other teachers did as well.'

'That's good,' he said, making an entry in his note-book.

'Why are you asking me these questions?' Zenobia enquired.

'Well, he has done something wrong. Tell me, does he visit you in Lenasia?'

'No. I have not seen him since last year.'

'Do you know of any group he was involved with?'

'No.'

'He never spoke to you about it?'

'No.'

'So you lost touch with him this year?'

'Yes.'

'Well, thank you very much. I am trying to get all the information I can from acquaintances of his. I don't think I shall bother you again. Please accept my apologies.'

Zenobia rose and left the office.

Mr Ashoka, who had been listening from behind the door in his secretary's office, now walked out quickly and entered his office from the front door.

'Thank you very much,' the colonel said. 'I have all the information I need.'

He shook Mr Ashoka's hand and walked out of the office. Mr Ashoka realised that he had not offered the man any tea. He hurried after him, but the colonel had already reached his car, so that when Mr Ashoka reached the gate the colonel accelerated away with a tyre-screeching thrust that left Mr Ashoka open-mouthed with shock.

He returned to his office and sat down. For a brief moment he felt a satisfying, vengeful thrill that Zenobia was a suspect in a conspiracy, but it was eclipsed by the thought that soon everyone would know of the interrogation, and that Ashoka High School would become notorious as a sanctuary for political dissidents. He might be accused by Security of being their patron.

Zenobia was not perturbed by the questioning, though a

little mystified that the colonel had decided to conduct the interview at school. She mentioned this to her two daughters, Mehroon and Soraya, at supper-time. (Kamar was away in Cape Town for a trial.)

'Perhaps he thought you would be psychologically unprepared and say something revealing,' Mehroon suggested. She was as tall as her mother, though her complexion was darker and her hair short.

'Or perhaps Tela has been arrested and gave your name as that of a friend,' Soraya said. She was fairly plump, smaller than her sister, her hair tied in two plaits.

'He spoke of Tela being involved with some group. I hope he is safe somewhere,' their mother said.

'You don't think Ashoka had anything to do with it?' Mehroon asked.

'No.'

'Why don't you telephone father and tell him,' Soraya said.

'It's not serious.'

Nothing further was said about the questioning, but late that night there was a knock on the front door and when Zenobia opened it she saw Colonel van der Spuy and two other men.

'We want to make a search,' he said.

'What for?'

'That's part of Security. Is your husband in?'

'No.'

The colonel walked in, followed by his assistants. They looked in the lounge, the dining-room, the kitchen, the bedrooms, where they opened the cupboard doors, the study and finally the bathroom and the toilet.

'If you are looking for Tela here,' Zenobia said as they

moved towards the lounge and front door, 'you will not find him.'

'I know that,' the colonel said, pausing for a moment at the door.

'Then why the search?'

'That's part of Security,' he answered, smiling faintly. 'Good night.'

Zenobia and her daughters sat in the lounge for a while feeling a little troubled and depressed.

'If the colonel suspected we were hiding Tela why did he question you at school?' Soraya asked her mother.

'It's all very mysterious.'

'Perhaps,' Mehroon said, 'he thought that after the questioning we would feel safe enough to hide Tela here.'

'This is not an age of reason,' Zenobia commented.

'I wish father was here,' Soraya sighed.

'There is nothing he could have done,' her mother said, taking her hand.

CHAPTER FIFTEEN

Soon after his meeting with Mr Ashoka, Prince Yusuf opened his perfume salon in downtown Johannesburg. He had spent large sums in order to have the façade and arched doorway ornamented with gold Islamic calligraphy and foliate patterns in multi-coloured mosaic. The upper half of the door was of opaque purple glass with a brilliant stained glass red rose in the centre. The interior of the salon radiated a soft aura of beauty and mystery, constrasting strongly with the carnival vulgarity of the other shops in the street.

There were no garish signs outside the perfume salon to tell the customer — a tall, blonde, blue-eyed lady with a cameo-smooth face by the Cosmetic House of Alexandra de Markoff, dressed in clothes by Pierre Cardin — what to expect within. She looked at the words 'Prince Yusuf's Perfume Salon' above the doorway, and the words released a vague yearning in her for the enchanted places of the East, for fountains where perfumes splashed among aquatic blooms, and nights of unending love. She pressed a button and the door opened automatically. She entered and saw an elegant black man with a forest of hair, dressed in tight, striped indigo pants and a pearl-grey shirt open in front, coming towards her. He bowed low and asked, 'Have you an appointment, madam?'

'No.'

'Let me see if I can fit you in for a consultation. Come with me.'

He went towards a reception desk, and asked the lady to be seated. He then sat down, took pen and pad and asked, 'Your name, please.'

'Karen Korda.'

He then opened another book, looked at some entries, picked up the telephone, pressed a button and spoke: 'Prince Yusuf, is it possible for you to have a consultation with Lady Karen Korda immediately? Madame Eleanor van der Byle telephoned a few minutes ago to postpone her appointment till tomorrow as an unexpected American visitor has arrived.'

'Yes.'

'Prince Yusuf,' the receptionist said, standing up and bowing, 'will be delighted to have a consultation with you immediately. Follow me, madam.'

Lady Karen Korda went through a curtained doorway, and down a thickly-carpeted narrow passage to reach emerald-green curtains which opened as she approached. The receptionist bowed and asked her to enter.

She found herself in a mysteriously lit room, the light seeming to emanate from ornate bottles of perfume — jade, roseate, amber — in two cabinets on either side. In the middle of the room, on a purple satin cushion, sat

Prince Yusuf, his crimson sandals beside him. He was dressed in a dark blue satin robe with a design of golden florets along the sleeve edges and on either side of the breast. His pants were 'antique' gold. His turban was peacock-green with a yellow onyx in the middle. His silken magenta-red shirt showed much of his manly torso.

'Sit down, Karen Korda,' he said in a pseudo-commanding tone. She sat down on a lilac cushion.

'I am pleased you have come to consult me,' he said in a musical, majestic voice. 'It will be a great pleasure for me to undertake the task of blending a unique perfume for a beautiful woman such as you, a gift of the divine . . . a perfume that shall have the redolence of your personality.'

The lady was fascinated by the handsome 'prince', debonair, charming, courteous, mysterious. The outside world of noisy cars, hurrying commonplace pedestrians, mercenary shopkeepers, evanesced from her memory.

'Thank you very much, Prince Yusuf,' Karen Korda said softly.

'Divine lady, do you prefer a synthetic perfume, or a natural perfume? Or a blend of the two?'

'I don't know much about perfumes.'

'Well, from my studies and research in the Orient, in the cities of Bokhara, Medina, Baghdad, Samarkand, Isfahan, Delhi, I have gained an entry into the arcane knowledge required in the preparation and blending of perfumes. A synthetic perfume is harsh, pungent, stringent, but has lasting qualities; while a natural perfume is soft, smooth, tranquil, but has transient qualities like true beauty.'

'I prefer a soft perfume.'

'Karen Korda, I am not sure. A perfume is a thing of beauty, but like beauty a thing of infinite complexity.

That is why purchasing a perfume off the shelf does not only display vulgar taste, but is disastrous to the total ensemble of a person. Look at it in this way. The best art is that where form (in this case the artificial perfume) is inseparably united to the content (in this case the natural perfume), the form holding, protecting and exalting the ephemeral. Therefore, a beautifully blended perfume is like a great work of art − like a play by Sophocles or Shakespeare, the Venus de Milo, a rare Persian carpet or the Taj Mahal - enhancing our sense of perfection and of the ideal. But just as we purchase a particular picture or sculpture so that it will do justice to a particular room or hall, so too a perfume must be intimately related to a person.'

The lady was charmed by Prince Yusuf's wisdom about perfumes and the mystique he radiated.

'Do you agree, Karen?'

'Of course.'

'Before I can blend a special perfume for you, you will appreciate that I will have to know you a shade more intimately. Buying and selling perfumes is not a vulgar commercial activity, but an art. A perfume is going to be resident in the human form and its quality must be closely related to the shape, colour and texture of every individual human form. That is why my perfumes are famous among the cultured and the sophisticated, because of their unique and subtle relation to the total human form. Will you come with me into the sanctum of the god of perfume so that I can make the necessary analysis that will help me in the distillation and blending of your own unique perfume?'

Prince Yusuf rose and the lady followed him through another curtain, down two steps, then through a door into a room.

In the middle of the room was a large, square bottle of smooth glass with an ornate neck and a spiral stopper. There was no furniture, only satin cushions on the blue and gold Persian carpet. Four large lattice-work copper pots stood in the corners.

Prince Yusuf stood for a moment beside the bottle, and asked Karen Korda to stand opposite him.

'Look into the heart of the bottle for a moment while I offer my prayers to the god of perfume, and supplicate him to guide me and inspire me with the knowledge required in the preparation of your blend.'

He stood in silence for some time, the palms of his hands pressed together and held before his face. He said a few words in a language the lady did not understand. Then he opened the stopper of the bottle. A perfume rose and filled the room with a delicate aroma. The lady felt, in the atmosphere of the room, that she had entered a casbah of enchantment and beauty, the magic sensual world of the Arabian Nights.

Prince Yusuf now sat down on a cushion, asked the lady to sit down before him, and took a pen and pad that were in a tray beside him.

'I am now,' he said, ' going to make an examination of your beauty and annotate the result of my analysis in the secret language of my profession. After you leave I shall meditate here until illumination comes to me on the various blends that will go into the formulation of your perfume. Tomorrow I shall distil the mixture in my laboratory and the following day you can collect it from my receptionist. Now, Karen Korda, will you please remove your scarf.'

The lady removed her scarf and Prince Yusuf made a note.

'Will you remove your blouse, please.'

The lady obliged unhesitatingly. She felt as though some invisible influence was in control of her hands.

Prince Yusuf made another entry and then requested she remove her brassière.

She removed a tiny clasp in front and her breasts emerged like luscious peeled fruit as the brassière parted.

'Now the rest.'

The lady stood up, unzipped and the garments fell at her feet. She sat down again.

'Now look into my eyes, Karen.'

Karen looked into Prince Yusuf's dark eyes. She saw a subdued light within, slowly brightening. She did not perceive a light within the perfume bottle increasing in intensity.

'Now relax and lie down upon the cushions, Karen Korda. Close your mind to every thought while I invoke the god of perfume to enter this room, examine your beautiful body, come into contact with it, and later illumine me in the preparation of your blend.'

Karen Korda lay down on the cushions and her consciousness metamorphosed into fragrance, redolent of orange blossom, gardenia bloom and tuberose.

CHAPTER SIXTEEN

One Saturday evening Mr Ashoka was in his study when he heard a loud knock on the front door of his house. Usually his wife or Deva opened the door to visitors, but this imperious summons brought him hurrying out of his study. He entered the lounge and opened the front door. It was Prince Yusuf.

'Mr Ashoka! How are you? I have been thinking of you almost every day this week. A friend of mine in Parktown wants to meet you. She is very interested in Indian culture. You must visit her palatial home.'

Mr Ashoka felt as though he were in the lady's palatial home already, instead of in his stereotyped government-planned house. The illusion was created by Prince Yusuf's appearance — his striped, plum-coloured suit, his pastel pink shirt, matching tie, tie pin and cuff links gleaming with wine-red gemstones, his gold watch, and ruby bejewelled fingers, the perfume that surrounded him like a second presence.

'You must come with me now in the Mustang. She is expecting you. I have told her all about you . . . .'

Mrs Ashoka stood with Deva in the kitchen doorway, fascinated by the visitor. Prince Yusuf saw her, went up to her and held her hand.

'I am so glad to meet you, Mrs Ashoka. I have just told your husband of a wealthy lady in Parktown who wants to meet a cultured Indian gentleman. Mr Ashoka is just the right person to talk to her.'

Deva tugged at Prince Yusuf's coat sleeve and said, 'I am sure you are not a teacher.'

'How do you know that?' Prince Yusuf asked.

'Teachers are born in the cemetery. They are ghosts.'

'Clever boy!' Prince Yusuf exclaimed, suddenly lifting him up in the air and putting him down. 'What is your name?'

'Deva.'

'Deva, do you want a gun?'

Prince Yusuf gave him his gun. Deva, delighted with it, began running round the room, laughing and shouting, 'I want to send my teacher back to the cemetery!'

'No Deva!' his father shouted, terrified that the boy would press the trigger. He ran after his son, who eluded him. Prince Yusuf laughed while Mrs Ashoka looked on, a little bewildered by the transformation of her lounge into a circus ring. Deva ran past Prince Yusuf who, with a deft flick of his fingers, snatched the gun from Deva's hand. Father and son fell in a heap on the floor.

'What fun!' Prince Yusuf said, lending a hand to Mr Ashoka. Then he put his arm around Deva and said, 'Run outside and sit in my Mustang. I am going to take you for a drive.' To Mr Ashoka he said, 'Get ready. I am coming back to fetch you in a few minutes.' He left the house and roared off in the Mustang with an excited Deva.

When they returned, Deva was happily holding Prince Yusuf's hand.

'You have a wonderful son,' Prince Yusuf said to Mr Ashoka who was now dressed in his best blue-grey suit. 'You should have seen how he enjoyed himself.' Mr Ashoka paid no attention to what Prince Yusuf said, but told his son that during his absence he should remain in the study and write a composition on 'A day in the life of a fisherman'.

Deva looked miserable.

'Write a composition on a Saturday night?' Prince Yusuf queried. 'But why not write a composition with the title, "The day I went for a drive in a friend's Mustang".'

Deva jumped and clapped his hands and cried, 'I will! I will!'

'I should have been a teacher,' Prince Yusuf said. 'I love children.' He patted Deva, telling the boy he would take him for a longer drive when he came to visit again. Deva ran happily to the study to write his composition, disregarding his father who was still mumbling something to him about 'serious work'.

Prince Yusuf said good-bye to Mrs Ashoka and the two men left the house. They climbed into the Mustang and sped away.

'Eleanor is waiting for you,' Prince Yusuf said. 'By the way, do you know anybody in Parktown or Hillbrow?'

'No,' Mr Ashoka replied.

'You never leave Lenasia, even during weekends?'

'I go to Durban during holidays.'

'That's once or twice a year. That's nothing. Which

night-club do you go to?'

'I have never been to a night-club,' Mr Ashoka confessed.

'Teachers are a strange lot,' Prince Yusuf said. 'They have so much time on hand and don't know what to do with it.'

'They spend their time in drinking saloons,' Mr Ashoka said jocosely, trying to match Prince Yusuf's gay mood.

'You are right,' Prince Yusuf said with a laugh.

'By the way, I owe you some money. It won't be long before I return it. I have just discovered a gold reef. But I owe others bigger sums which I want to return first. You don't mind.'

'Not at all,' Mr Ashoka replied, not wanting to think about money in the company of a genial friend and powerful ally.

The Mustang turned onto a moonlit highway and flew over it with the swiftness of Pegasus. Prince Yusuf offered Mr Ashoka a cigarette and the two men enjoyed their smoking while watching the receding lights on either side of the road.

The car soon reached Parktown, raced through a street of magnificent, gracious homes set among gardens and huge trees, then turned into a driveway and brought them to the entrance of a Tudor-style house.

Prince Yusuf jumped out of the car and, coming over to Mr Ashoka's side, opened the door for him. 'You are going to meet a very wealthy lady,' he said as they walked up the steps towards the entrance of the house, where bougain-villeas bloomed in two large pots. Prince Yusuf pressed the bell-button and the maid appeared.

'Hullo Phyllis, tell the madam we are here,' Prince Yusuf said, leading the way through a carpeted entrance hall where exotic plants grew in pots, to a spacious lounge where tapestry hung along the walls beside precious paintings. Antique furniture glowed with a mellow sheen under the light from two ornate chandeliers, and rare Persian carpets lay on the floor among velvet cushions.

'Sit down, Mr Ashoka,' Prince Yusuf said,' while I pour your drink. What will you have?' He opened a cabinet.

'A red wine will do.'

'Ah, wonderful. I will have one too.'

'Make it three,' a dry voice said, as Eleanor emerged from the doorway. A childless widow in her late thirties, she was 'as graceful as a minaret' (a descriptive phrase used by Prince Yusuf in a romantic moment); her complexion a rich bronze acquired through long hours of exposure beside the swimming pool in the rear garden of her home; her soft, dyed ash-blonde hair was artistically piled by the hair-dresser above her rather angular face. Her dress, designed in Italy by the fashion house of Pucci (even the furniture and the tapestry had been sent from Rome by Pucci) was of lustrous 'antique' green material, slit down to the hem on the right side. The perfume that enveloped her was from Prince Yusuf's Perfume Salon, a shop that was becoming a favourite among society ladies.

'This is Mr Ashoka,' Prince Yusuf said as Eleanor came up. Mr Ashoka stood up to be introduced. Eleanor held Mr Ashoka's hand for a while and said, 'Prince Yusuf told me all about you. All my life I have been dying to meet a learned Indian gentleman. You belong to a cultured race of such ancient lineage that I can only tremble in your presence.'

'Here, Eleanor, this will stop you from trembling,' Prince Yusuf said, handing her a goblet of wine. He handed another to Mr Ashoka.

Eleanor laughed with delight.

'Let us drink,' she said, holding her goblet up towards the chandelier, 'to the glorious culture of the Orient.'

They sipped a mouthful and then heard the doorbell ring.

'That's Charmaine and Cordell and Anne-Marie,' Eleanor said. 'They have come to meet you, Mr Ashoka. There they are. Come in.'

The three women had arrived in a Mercedez Benz. They were dressed in clothing from Christian Dior; their faces were the products of the cosmetic laboratories of Lancome, Juvena, Fameux. Their perfume, too, had come from the salon of Prince Yusuf. Charmaine was a small woman whose short, thick, brown hair seemed to have been coiffured by a taxidermist, her body formed by a confectioner. She wore a white lace blouse and a pale blue skirt with matching shoes. Cordell was of medium height, her figure betraying a food habit which alternated between bouts of gorging and starvation. She wore straight purple trousers and a vivid cerise dress. Anne-Marie was the best looking of the trio: her hair was a winter sun, her eyes Chinese jade, her body a ballerina's. She was dressed in a knitted black georgette one-shoulder dress with an exotic palm leaf embellishing the front.

Eleanor introduced Mr Ashoka to the three ladies as 'my dear friend, in whose classically-moulded head the glorious culture of the Orient is enshrined.' The three ladies shook hands with Mr Ashoka, admiring his facial features and shining wavy hair.

'Are you an untouchable?' Eleanor asked.

Mr Ashoka winced momentarily.

'You must be,' Cordell said. 'I can see it in your eyes.'

'Wine, pretty ladies,' Prince Yusuf intervened, with goblets on a tray. Each took a glass and Eleanor again lifted hers to the chandelier and proposed a toast in celebration of the Orient and 'its distinguished representative Mr Ashoka.'

After that everyone sat down on cushions scattered on the Persian carpets (an arrangement Eleanor had copied from Prince Yusuf's salon). Eleanor sat cross-legged near Mr Ashoka; the three other ladies reclined beside Prince Yusuf.

Eleanor struck a gong near her. At once Phyllis and two other servants — clad in white tunics like nurses, but wearing blue turbans — came into the room. They placed several small tables within reach of the guests and left; then returned with trolleys laden with trays of hors d'oeuvres and party fare: smoked angel fish, beef fillet simmered in Burgundy sauce, lentil salad with sausages and mushrooms, olives from Greece, asparagus, a variety of cheese and bottles of wine. They served the guests.

'Tell me, Mr Ashoka,' Eleanor asked, licking avocado dip mantling an asparagus, 'are you a sufi? I am just crazy about them. You know the whole idea of going into the bush naked and receiving the infinite in one's arms.'

'I am a worshipper of Krishna,' Mr Ashoka replied.

'Oh how wonderful!' Anne-Marie cried. 'When I was in London last year I bought a picture from a holy man in a saffron-coloured robe. It was of Krishna among . . . among . . . .'

'Gopis, milk-maids,' Mr Ashoka helped her.

'Oh how wonderful to be Krishna's milk-maid!' Cordell yearned.

'Gopi is more romantic,' Prince Yusuf suggested.

'What a lovely word instead of the vulgar milkmaid!' Eleanor said. 'I wish I were a gopi. I would then be able to do all those divine Indian dances. Does your wife dance, Mr Ashoka? Oh, how foolish can I be? All Indian women are born dancers. I must go to India to see Krishna and the gopis dance.' She lifted one of her knees and her split dress fell apart in her lap, revealing a nylon-meshed leg. Mr Ashoka looked up modestly at the chandelier for a moment.

'Krishna lived many years ago, my dear,' Prince Yusuf corrected.

'He is eternally there for me, dancing with the gopis,' Eleanor said, lifting a goblet of roseate wine to her lips.

'He lives in the eternal mind,' Mr Ashoka philosophised.

Everyone was silent for a moment as though trying to grasp the nature of metaphysical truth.

'Oh, how modern Krishna was, enjoying himself among the gopis,' Charmaine brought them back to earth, placing one leg over Prince Yusuf's lap and eating crayfish and mushroom cocktail.

'Because we Easterners are so ancient and modern at the same time, we know the art of living,' Prince Yusuf said, like a connoisseur.

'You certainly do, my Persian prince,' Anne-Marie sighed, placing her jewelled hand on his shoulder.

'I am sure Krishna was a friend of the sufis,' Eleanor commented, giving Mr Ashoka some salad from a tray. 'Perhaps he learnt about the gopis from them. Prince Yusuf, doesn't your favourite poet Hafiz — or is it Omar Khayyam — speak of thou and I in the wilderness, or something like that? You Indians are marvellous poets.'

'Hafiz and Omar Khayyam are Persians,' Prince Yusuf

reminded her.

'Persians, Indians, you are all the same, coming from the divine Orient.'

Prince Yusuf sipped wine and recited a verse from Hafiz:

' "Say further, sweetheart wind, when thus thou blowest;
 What but thy little girdle of woven gold
 Should the firm centre of my hopes enfold?
 Thy legendary waist does it not hold,
 And mystic treasures which thou only knowest?" '

'You Easterners have no sense of sin. Isn't that wonderful!' Anne-Marie said languidly, lying outstretched on a velvet cushion.

'No transgressions, no confessions,' Prince Yusuf said and the ladies laughed with delight.

'How beautiful your women are!' Eleanor extolled, placing a cigarette in a long holder, stretching her legs out and reclining on one elbow. 'They are so naturally elegant. How nymph-like they look in their saris. Prince Yusuf has given me a dozen and I can't get used to one.'

'The sari is so poetic,' Cordell rhapsodized. 'But it is not for us, the sinful daughters of the fallen Eve.'

'Just as well,' Prince Yusuf added. 'You can imagine the trouble I would have had in unwinding it.'

The women laughed merrily and Mr Ashoka smiled. Charmaine stood up, poured wine into everyone's goblets and Prince Yusuf recited a stanza from the Rubaiyat:

' "Ah, my Belovèd, fill the cup that clears
 To-day of past Regrets and future Fears —
 To-morrow? — Why, To-morrow I may be
 Myself with Yesterday's Sev 'n Thousand Years." '

Everyone was charmed and Anné-Marie stretched herself

out on the cushion in surrender and sighed, 'Beautiful! Beautiful!'

'Now, Mr Ashoka,' Prince Yusuf said, 'it is your turn. Let the ladies hear you discourse on Hindu religion and philosophy.'

Mr Ashoka sat up, crossed his legs guru-wise and began to speak of the philosophy of the Gita and the Upanishads. Then he elaborated on the mythology and the creation of the deities of the Hindu pantheon, and ended his long discourse by quoting Krishna's words to Arjuna in the Gita:

' "The sense-instruments, they say, are high; higher than the sense-instruments is the mind; higher than mind is the understanding; but higher than understanding is Self." '

Everyone was quiet for a while as though meditating on the truth of the words.

'Listen to the poet Jami,' Prince Yusuf said:
' "Drink deep of earthly love, that so thy lip
   May learn the wine of holier love to sip." '

'How lovely!' Anne-Marie cried rapturously. 'Even Shakespeare could not have composed a more honeyed couplet.'

Then Eleanor asked, 'Tell me, Mr Ashoka, what is your first name?'

'Dharma.'

'Dharma. How beautiful! Prince Yusuf tells me all Eastern names have meaning. What is yours?'

'It has several meanings. Truth and duty are two.'

'How divine that a name should have several meanings,' Eleanor said. 'I can see truth in your eyes, my dear Dharma. I shall be your disciple and learn truth at your feet.' She put her glass to her lips and drank all the wine, flinging her head back in bacchanalian abandonment.

'Eleanor,' Prince Yusuf enquired, 'have I lost you?'

'Yes, eternally,' she replied, filling her goblet from a nearby bottle.

'How wonderful to be in a harem,' Anne-Marie yearned, biting a toasted buttered roll, laden with grilled shrimp, 'to be bathed in perfumed water by jewelled black eunuchs and have poets read their poetry to you. I wish I lived in Arabia.'

'Drink some wine and drown your sorrow,' Prince Yusuf comforted her, pouring wine into her goblet, 'for Persia's Omar says:

"Drink wine by moonlight, O Love! for the moon
  Will often shine hereafter and will not find us!" '

Anne-Marie held up her goblet with both hands and then drank slowly, tilting her head back as far as it could go.

'Tell me, Dharma,' Eleanor asked, leaning on one elbow and placing her cigarette holder on the edge of an opal ash-tray, 'are you really an untouchable?'

Prince Yusuf put his arm around Cordell's shoulders and waited amusedly to hear his answer. He saw Mr Ashoka's face harden implacably.

'Oh, how stupid of me even to ask the question,' Eleanor went on. 'Of course everyone can see you are an untouchable. Your noble caste shines through you.'

Prince Yusuf saw Mr Ashoka's face relax. 'The caste system does not operate in this country,' Mr Ashoka reminded her.

'Of course not, my dear Dharma. In this country fine natural distinctions have been destroyed by crude racial divisions. How rotten this country must be to you, discriminated against daily, herded into corrals and bullied by every tramp with a white skin.'

'My religion teaches patience,' Mr Ashoka said in a lofty tone.

'How your religion stands up to us! How thoroughly uncivilised we are!' Eleanor cried.

Mr Ashoka smiled and looked at the ladies. There was no point in taking them seriously. They were merely playthings. Their end in life was to amuse themselves and others. Purposeful living meant nothing to them.

'Ladies,' Prince Yusuf said, 'Mr Ashoka may perhaps be the descendant of the famous emperor Ashoka who lived in the third century B.C. in India. When I was in India a few years ago I saw one of his stone capitals on which his moral edicts appear. The emperor was a follower of the Buddha.'

The ladies looked at Mr Ashoka as though he were the emperor himself.

Prince Yusuf took a bottle of wine and asked everyone to hold their goblets near him. When the crystal goblets glowed with ruby vintage, he said, 'Mr Ashoka is a very important man in Lenasia. He is headmaster of a school named after him.'

'How wonderful!' Charmaine, Cordell and Anne-Marie cried in a chorus.

'That is a great honour indeed,' Eleanor said, 'to have a school named after you in your lifetime. Most of us poor mortals are only thought of, if at all, after we are dead. That is our fate, I suppose. We drink to you, Mr Ashoka.'

Everyone took a sip of liquor.

'Listen,' Prince Yusuf said, 'to Hafiz:

"Speak not of fate; ah! change the theme,

114

And talk of odours, talk of wine,
Talk of the flowers that round us bloom:
'Tis all a cloud, 'tis all a dream;
To love and joy thy thoughts confine
Nor hope to pierce the sacred gloom." '

Everyone applauded Prince Yusuf's talent for reciting poetry. He now rose from the carpet, put a dance record on the hi-fi set and taking Anne-Marie in his arms began to dance. He was a master at ball-room dancing. The others watched the dancing couple for a while.

'Let me dance with you, my dear Dharma,' Eleanor said, taking his hand.

'I don't dance.'

'You have never danced in your life?'

'I have always been involved in studies.'

'Oh noble soul! Dear Dharma, please forgive me for trying to corrupt you. I am merely a daughter of the sinful Eve. I might as well go on sinning, since I am doomed anyway.'

She went towards Prince Yusuf, dispossessed him of Anne-Marie and danced a tango with him. Mr Ashoka, reclining beside three women, felt like an emperor in his harem.

As soon as the dance ended, Eleanor, pointing to the door with outstretched hand, said in a commanding voice, 'To the swimming pool!'

The three women beside Mr Ashoka jumped up and followed Eleanor out of the room. Prince Yusuf and Mr Ashoka, who felt a little disappointed that the women had left his side, followed.

The swimming pool was at the back of the house, a beautiful blue heart-shaped jewel lit up from within. A

115

variety of trees and flowering shrubs, softly glazed by the light from the pool, enclosed it on all sides. Mr Ashoka could not swim, so he sat in a wrought-iron outdoor chair and watched the others. Phyllis brought wine and delicacies for him.

Prince Yusuf and the ladies dived into the pool. After swimming for a while they played with a ball and Mr Ashoka, sitting under a magnolia, was forgotten. He dozed off for a short period and when he opened his eyes they were still playing in the water, though they seemed to be receding away from him. He fell asleep . . . .

Phyllis came to him and said, 'Come, my master, I want to lead you to the cave of pleasure. Follow me.' He rose and walked behind her. She was still dressed in her white uniform and turban. She walked on without looking behind. She led him to the back of the mansion, to a little thatch-roofed hut hidden among bamboos and the trunks of dead trees. She opened the door and went in. Mr Ashoka, corded by fear but impelled by desire, entered the oblong darkness. Suddenly a light bulb flashed and he saw stretched out on a servant's steel bed Phyllis, naked, with only her turban on. The light went off and then went on almost instantly again. He saw, standing in the doorway, Prince Yusuf and the ladies, looking at him coiled in Phyllis's legs and arms.

Eleanor came closer, pointed a tragedienne's finger at him and said, 'There lies the glorious Orient in ruins.' The others recoiled in disgust and horror.

He awoke in a sweat and saw Prince Yusuf and a quartet of naiads in the swimming pool. Prince Yusuf was holding aloft a ball with one hand and the naiads were laughing merrily and trying to grab the ball from him; he flung the ball out of the pool towards Mr Ashoka. It fell neatly on the middle of his head and spattered him with water, then rebounded on the lawn and disappeared in the shrubbery.

Prince Yusuf and the ladies laughed as they emerged from the pool and dried themselves with towels. After they had changed clothing they came over to Mr Ashoka. It was time to leave.

As they walked towards the cars Eleanor, whose voice sounded drier after her swim, said, 'Dear Dharma, I am planning to go with Prince Yusuf and my three darlings to the Polana during the long weekend. You must come with us. There you shall have your cabaret and caviar . . . .'

'Tennis and barbecue . . . ' chimed Charmaine.

'Casino and haute cuisine . . . ' sang Ann-Marie.

'Bed and gopi,' predicted Prince Yusuf, and everyone laughed joyfully.

The three ladies departed first, after shaking Mr Ashoka's hand and kissing Eleanor and Prince Yusuf. Then Prince Yusuf and Mr Ashoka took their leave of Eleanor, who kissed them both on their foreheads. As the car swung into the street from the driveway, Mr Ashoka looked back and saw Eleanor standing with uplifted arms before her mansion as though she were supplicating the stars for something.

On the way home Mr Ashoka said: 'Isn't it strange that Europeans are so ignorant of Eastern civilisations and culture?'

'Western conquerors,' Prince Yusuf replied, 'if they did not destroy, seldom learnt anything because of conceit about their superiority.'

CHAPTER SEVENTEEN

It was a Saturday afternoon when Mr Ashoka and his wife went to the Ramakrishna Hall to attend a wedding ceremony (Deva, not being interested in weddings had been sent to the cinema). An old pupil of the school had invited them to 'grace his marriage' by their attendance.

When Mr and Mrs Ashoka entered the hall they were received by usherettes in parrot-bright saris. A band was playing below the stage and a man was singing a love song from a recent Indian film. On the stage — against a background of blue, green, orange and yellow crinkle paper stretched from floor to ceiling — stood a wooden pavilion ornamented with gold and silver foil and multi-coloured globes. The front of the stage was lined with burning wicks in little brass vessels. In the centre of the pavilion was a large black pot in which the sacred fire would be lit when the priest arrived to conduct the wedding ceremony.

When the song was over someone announced that Dr Zia would speak to the guests. He came on the stage (his new

Mercedes Benz was parked outside the main entrance of the hall) and began reading his speech: 'We are gathered here on this stupendous occasion to witness the primordial ceremony devised and implemented by our illustrious ancestors in these luminous precincts to reveal to man that marriage is a risk, a risk taken by man . . . . ' The doctor was followed by another doctor (he too had his new Mercedes Benz outside) who spoke of marriage as 'an exchange transplant of two hearts, and such a transplant has a greater chance of success than anything that mortal hands of surgeons can do . . . .'

When the doctor had finished, Mr Ashoka was called upon to address the guests. He was flustered for a moment, but, quickly regaining his composure, walked towards the stage. An adept at making public speeches, he went on to speak of marriage as 'an extension of the educational process . . . .' He ended by wishing, on behalf of the guests, the bride and bridegroom a very happy life together (voicing a sentiment the medical men had overlooked).

Several women now came on the stage carrying bowls containing rice, camphor, incense, melted butter, and platters laden with coconuts, marigolds, banana leaves and jars of water. The singer now began a hymn from the Rig Veda to the accompaniment of a lone sitar. More women in luminous saris came on the stage. Some stood around the pavilion and others within. Then the priest entered, a small man in a modern suit, looking inconspicuous amid all the finery and brilliance. He began reading from the Gita.

Mr Ashoka listened intently and when he heard the priest utter Lord Krishna's words that 'All living creatures are led astray as soon as they are born, by the delusion that this relative world is real', he felt as though the god was addressing the words to him personally. The world was not real. Was that not a substantial consolation to him? Let all those who had opposed him since he began to undertake the responsibility of administering a school go on opposing him. The world was not real. It was like the pavilion in which the priest was standing. After the wedding it would be dismantled; all the coloured paper and foil stripped, and the lights extinguished.

As soon as the priest had finished the bride entered accompanied by her family and a retinue of women. She was dressed in a red sari and lavishly ornamented with gold jewellery. Then the bridegroom entered, accompanied by his family. He was dressed in a fawn suit and wore a Nehru cap. The bride approached the bridegroom, welcomed him with a garland, then dipped her finger in a little bowl held by an attendant maiden, and imprinted a red dot on his forehead. The couple entered the pavilion where the sacred fire had now been lit in the pot. While the priest uttered the marriage vows, the bridal couple emptied into the pot the ritual offerings from the bowls and platters placed near them. The bride's mother led her to a flat stone; the bride placed her foot on it and her mother reminded her of her conjugal responsibilities. The priest tied the end of the bride's sari to a handkerchief in the bridegroom's hand. The couple took seven steps around the sacred fire, while the priest intoned ceremonial prayers and holy water was splashed on the couple, blessing their union.

They were now congratulated by the people on the stage and then by all the guests. Those who had brought gifts handed them to a man entrusted to collect them.

Mr and Mrs Ashoka went over to wish the married pair a happy life together. The bridegroom — tall, handsome —

took the opportunity of inviting Mr Ashoka to a special reception at his home during the evening. Then Mr and Mrs Ashoka went to the adjoining dining hall where they were served food.

Later he took his wife home. In the evening he set off in his car for the bridegroom's home, leaving his wife to look after Deva.

Mr Ashoka was welcomed by the bridegroom, Kanti, and led into the lounge where there were several other guests. While he was speaking to two men he knew, he saw a very handsome man in the corner of the room, bending over a table pouring liquor into glasses on a tray. He recognised him immediately by his clothing: Prince Yusuf. He was dressed in a dark blue suit with a matching tie and shirt. His wrists gleamed with a silver watch and sapphire-inset cuff links. The large ring on his finger scintillated. 'That's a diamond,' Mr Ashoka heard a whisper within him, 'perhaps bought with the money I lent him.'

Prince Yusuf came with the tray of drinks and put it on a glass table in the centre of the room. When he lifted up his head to announce to the guests that drinks were poured, he saw Mr Ashoka. 'Aha!' he exclaimed, 'my friend Mr Ashoka.' He went up to his friend, shook his hand and said to the guests, 'Gentlemen, you all heard Mr Ashoka deliver that wonderful speech in the hall. If you have not yet met him, please do so now.' Some of the guests came up and shook hands. 'Now, gentlemen,' Prince Yusuf continued, 'please take a glass of liquor.' Everyone came up to the table, took a glass, and Prince Yusuf proposed a toast to Kanti, wishing him joy and happiness in his married life.

After the toast Prince Yusuf sat down on a chair near

Mr Ashoka and said, 'Tell me, how is your school getting on? It must be wonderful. I wish I were a teacher. And tell me, how did you enjoy the evening in Parktown? Eleanor cannot stop talking about you . . . .'

The gush of words that flowed from his lips was so charming that Mr Ashoka no longer thought of the money he had lent Prince Yusuf, though the diamond on his finger never ceased scintillating. Kanti moved among the guests. When he came up to them, Prince Yusuf remarked that if Mr Ashoka's school produced men like Kanti, then it was the finest school in the world.

Women came in and served the guests with a variety of delicacies. As time passed, more liquor was consumed and the guests became a little noisier. At intervals Kanti was called away by the women in another part of the house. There was much talk among the men. A Mr Naidu — he was the secretary of a trade union in Durban — was speaking on the struggle of the proletariat against 'capitalist and middle-class hegemony'. He went on: 'And things are not made easy for us by schools, for they teach middle-class employer values. We have a headmaster here. He can tell us whether I am speaking the truth or not.' Mr Naidu emptied his glass of liquor.

Someone told Mr Ashoka that he was being spoken to, and he turned towards Mr Naidu.

'Don't you teach middle-class employer values . . . headmaster?' Mr Naidu asked.

'I don't understand what you mean,' Mr Ashoka replied, putting his empty liquor glass on a side table. Prince Yusuf promptly refilled it and gave it back to him. He also filled Mr Naidu's glass.

'What I mean . . . is what I mean,' Mr Naidu said,

bending forward.

'I don't understand,' Mr Ashoka said.

'Does . . . does headmaster look like a worker?' Mr Naidu asked the other guests.

'Of course,' Prince Yusuf replied, enjoying the argument, 'teachers are workers. They don't earn half as much as trade union officials.'

Mr Naidu, who was a very short man with a small face and thick hair, much of it falling like a black wing across the right side of his forehead, pondered over the answer for a moment and then took a drink of liquor. Then, pointing a finger at Mr Ashoka, he said, 'Look at that headmaster. Does he look . . . like a worker? He has a bourgeois mentality . . . bourgeois mentality.'

'What do you mean?' Mr Ashoka asked, drinking liquor to stifle his irritation.

'What do I mean? Tell me . . . are you a worker . . . in the classical sense?'

Mr Ashoka was at a loss for an answer and drank more liquor.

'Mr Naidu,' Prince Yusuf interposed, 'you are being unfair to my friend, Mr Ashoka. Are you a worker in the classical sense?'

'Headmaster . . . your friend? Impossible! He is the government's friend . . . . He daily sells us down the drain . . . garlanding inspectors . . . raising the government's flag.'

The accusation struck Mr Ashoka and for a moment he experienced complete lucidity. He felt threatened and looked at Prince Yusuf for help.

'Let headmaster deny it!' Mr Naidu shouted, standing up, holding the glass of liquor obliquely in his hand and nearly falling forward. A friend grabbed him by the shoulder and made him sit again.

'All right, we shall settle the matter in a duel,' Prince Yusuf said, taking out his gun and pushing it across the low glass table. It came to a stop perilously near the edge of the table, close to Mr Naidu. 'Mr Naidu,' Prince Yusuf said, 'you shoot first and then it will be Mr Ashoka's turn.'

'If . . . if I kill headmaster . . . it will be a wasted bullet,' Mr Naidu said, and everyone burst into laughter.

Mr Ashoka decided to ignore Mr Naidu and spoke to a man near him.

'Capitalist stooge!' Mr Naidu shouted, becoming very agitated.

'Here, Mr Ashoka, take the gun and blow his proletarian brains out,' Prince Yusuf said laughingly. 'It's your turn now.'

'Stooge! Let him!' Mr Naidu shouted, trying to get up from his seat and shaking his index finger.

'I think I must go,' Mr Ashoka heard his own voice say, and he walked out of the room, trying to keep his legs as steady as possible.

'You are running away, capitalist stooge!' Mr Naidu's voice triumphed behind him.

Once outside, anger, bitterness and humiliation rose within him. His anger was not against Mr Naidu, but against Prince Yusuf who had stoked up the argument for his own amusement. After taking his five hundred rands, he had the audacity to enjoy himself at his expense. In spite of his appearance, he was nothing other than a scoundrel and a rogue. He had taken him to Parktown and there made him pollute himself with a black servant in a hut while he frolicked with white women in a swimming pool.

Mr Ashoka looked for his car in the street but did not
see it. He crossed the street and walked towards a vacant
plot of ground where a number of cars were parked. He
saw a car that he recognised, looking like a silver wraith in
the light of a street lamp. He went up to it and banged his
fists on the bonnet, exclaiming, 'My car! My car! He paid
for it with my money. Swindler! I will get my money back
from you!' He banged his fists once more on the Mustang
and walked from car to car looking for his own, but did
not find it. At last his key matched a lock. He got in,
started the car and drove off. But it seemed that someone
had played chess with the houses and buildings in the
suburb, and even turned the chess board around, so that
Nirvana Drive was now in the south instead of the north.
He drove around in a labyrinth and it was only when he
reached the sports stadium that he regained his bearings
and drove homewards.

Mr Ashoka's mind became prey to an irrational idea: he
was convinced Prince Yusuf had made an attempt on
his life by producing his gun at Kanti's party and urging
him to engage in a duel with Mr Naidu. It was a subtle way
of having him killed, so that Prince Yusuf need not pay
back the money he owed. The idea became an obsession
with him, disturbing him at intervals throughout the day.
At night was added another obsession: he was polluted.
The dream beside the swimming pool hardened into a
dimension of experiential reality. The genesis of both
obsessions, buried within his subconscious mind, lay in his
creeping paranoia, and the envy of the life of an extremely
handsome and fortunate man, living in bliss, surrounded

by a harem of beautiful women.

One of the mainsprings of Mr Ashoka's teaching career was to seek promotion, which in turn would bring a bigger monthly pay cheque. He now stood poorer by a sum of five hundred rands. He counted the number of things he could have bought with the money: he could have refurnished his lounge, or obtained a holiday air-ticket, or ordered a hundred bottles of the best liquor, or bought five new suits that would have matched Prince Yusuf's. Prince Yusuf had miscalculated if he thought he could make a profession out of swindling others. He, Ashoka, would check him. He would track him down and confront him.

Prince Yusuf had told him that he lived in Lenasia, but that was probably a lie as he had never told him where. He had also mentioned that his cousin's children attended his school, but that was probably also a lie. He could easily obtain his address from Kanti, but after some thought he decided against it as it could lead to a resurrection of the entire unpleasant incident when he had to 'run like a rat'. The simile thrust itself into his mind, strengthening his determination to retrieve his money. But perhaps he should see officer Ayer first and get his opinion. He went.

'Sit down, Mr Ashoka,' the officer said. 'I hope you have no problems with Deva.'

'No, sir. My problem is with a notorious swindler.'

He told the officer.

'There is nothing we can do,' the officer said regretfully after listening to his story. 'There is no evidence that can stand up in court. He can claim that he lent you the money and you returned it to him by giving him a cheque.'

'What can I do to get back my money?'

'Well, go to him and ask him for it.'

'He is a criminal.'

'Not yet. You have made no demand for the money. He may pay you.'

'There is one other thing. The man carries a gun.'

'He may have a permit.'

'Do you think he would use it if I demanded my money?'

'No sensible man would want to hang for five hundred rands, Mr Ashoka. I think if you ask him for the money you will get it.'

Mr Ashoka left, feeling that officer Ayer had been unhelpful. No doubt he had never been swindled himself. But he was determined to get his money back. He did not have Prince Yusuf's address, but he could perhaps obtain it from the steward at the bar in Fordsburg. He was about to go there in his car, when the thought occurred that the steward was probably in the pay of the swindler and would not give it to him. Perhaps if he visited all the bars in Lenasia during the late evening, he would see the Mustang outside one of them. He would wait outside in his car until the swindler came out. Then he would follow the Mustang and confront the man in his own house. If he failed to find him in Lenasia, he would go to the bar in Fordsburg and wait for him there.

Several evenings in succession Mr Ashoka visited the bars but failed to see the Mustang. Then one Saturday evening he saw the car and was filled with elation. He chuckled, 'I've got him.' He parked his own car nearby and watched for over an hour. The temptation grew in him to go to the doorway of the bar and have a look at what the man was doing: the notion came to him that the man was dispensing free drinks and telling everyone how he had taken five hundred rands from a school principal.

He climbed out of his car and went to the bar. The time was nearing ten o'clock and there was no one in the street. He stood in the doorway and had a quick look inside. There were three men sitting at the counter drinking, and he heard voices coming from the curtained-off part of the bar where the billiard table was. He entered the bar, sat down at the counter and ordered brandy. From where he sat he could see the edge of the billiard table and a player standing next to it with a cue in hand. The player moved away and Prince Yusuf became visible. He was dressed in a dark purple suit, a deep lilac shirt, a matching tie with tie pin and cuff links gleaming with mauve gems. As he stood there examining the positions of the billiard balls on the table and chalking his cue, Mr Ashoka saw a large flashing amethyst ring on his finger. 'With my money,' he heard himself whisper.

'This time the game is over,' Prince Yusuf said, bending over and taking aim.

He smacked the white ball with his cue; three other balls collided with each other, rebounded from the edge of the table and met their doom in the awaiting net in the corner.

'One more game,' Prince Yusuf said, 'and then it's home time.'

Mr Ashoka drank his brandy quickly, paid, and left the bar. He went to his car and waited.

After half an hour Prince Yusuf came out of the doorway of the bar, got into his Mustang, started it, and drove off. Mr Ashoka followed him. Fortunately for him Prince Yusuf did live in Lenasia and had no reason to drive at speed. Very soon he turned into a driveway leading to a double-storey house and Mr Ashoka drove past. Now he knew where the man lived. He would confront the swindler the next day.

Mr Ashoka went to Prince Yusuf's house at about eleven o'clock. It being Sunday, he reasoned that the swindler would not be up until then, considering the depraved sort of existence he led. When he knocked at the door an elderly lady opened it. He asked to see Prince Yusuf and the lady said that he had gone to visit his cousin in Lenasia.

'I must see him immediately,' Mr Ashoka said, fearing that if he did not get his money then, he never would later. 'It is very urgent.'

The lady told him the address and Mr Ashoka returned to his car. He would track down the man and demand his money and tell him what he thought of him. It didn't matter if others were present. In fact the embarrassment would expose him to others. He kept a gun in order to scare those he had swindled, but he, Mr Ashoka, was not afraid of him. The noisy engine of his car wound up his fury. He saw the Mustang and stopped sharply behind it. He got out of his car in a hurry, entered the gate and went towards the front door. He knocked. A young girl opened the door and Mr Ashoka entered without speaking. He saw Prince Yusuf sitting on a settee, smoking a cigar.

'You swindler, where is the money I gave you?' he shouted. 'You cheated me and then had the nerve to turn against me. You think that you can frighten me with your gun, you thief . . . !'

Prince Yusuf went on smoking calmly.

'Did you not take my five hundred rands? Who do you think you are? I put my trust in you and . . . .'

Out of the corner of his eye Mr Ashoka saw a lady appear

on his left. He turned to her. 'Lady, this man took my money and does not want to pay back,' he said.

The lady was tall, long-haired and dressed in denim jeans and a blouse. 'Who are you? Why are you shouting in this manner in my house?' she asked.

'Please excuse me . . . . '

The lady moved towards the door.

'Please leave this house immediately.'

'I am sorry . . . . '

'Will you get out. How embarrassing! Look at the people outside.'

She held the door open for him to leave.

Mr Ashoka walked out, head bowed. Several neighbours had come to the gate, wondering what was happening. They looked at Mr Ashoka as he passed by. Some recognised him and murmured his name.

As he got into his car Prince Yusuf came to the window and threw a piece of paper at him which fell on his lap. Mr Ashoka picked it up and, without looking at it, put it on the seat beside him. He drove away.

When he reached home he looked at the piece of paper. It was a cheque for one thousand rands. He looked at the cheque for a long while, mystified. Had Prince Yusuf forgotten how much he had taken from him? Or had he deliberately given him a cheque for twice the sum? Why should he have done so? Perhaps to checkmate him, for he could not now cash the cheque without feeling guilt-ridden, nor could he claim that Prince Yusuf owed him money. Locked in disappointment, he kept to his study for many hours. For the second time now he had been humiliated and forced to leave a house in the most ignominious manner. Should he go to apologise to the lady? The fear that he might be asked to leave again kept him at home.

Later, whenever he brooded on what had happened, he began to see the lady as Zenobia. Only Zenobia, who hated him, could have turned him out. He had been blinded by his fury at the time and had not seen the lady clearly; now his mind was lost in the labyrinth of his fantasy.

CHAPTER EIGHTEEN

One morning Mr Ashoka received a telephone call from Dr Whitecross who informed him that the Director of Education had arrived in the city on a brief visit and had expressed his desire to see the school, as he had heard how efficiently it was being run.

'We shall all be very highly honoured,' Mr Ashoka responded. But as a dark thought mushroomed in his mind, he went on, 'It has always been my intention to extend an invitation to you and the Director. The time has now arrived. But in order to make it a great and memorable occasion I must speak to the Parents' Committee. I will contact you again later when we have settled on something.'

As soon as he returned the telephone to its cradle the dark thought assumed visual definition: he saw a protest demonstration, led by Zenobia and her lackeys, holding aloft derisive placards. If that happened it could spell the end of his career in the educational world.

After much thought, he decided that it would be best to

invite the Director and the inspector to a private banquet during the evening in the school hall. He would ask the Parents' Committee to arrange the banquet to which only selected guests would be invited. He would make the Disciplinary Committee responsible for security. He would also ask officer Ayer to provide a police patrol. A very important State official was coming and every precaution had to be taken so that he would not be dishonoured or embarrassed in any way.

He then telephoned Dr Raj, told him of the Director's visit, and of his plan to make it a memorable one. Dr Raj replied that he felt certain that the Parents' Committee would agree to holding a banquet. Mr Ashoka went on to say, 'The Parents' Committee need not go to the expense of inviting all the teachers. We shall keep it a small exclusive affair and invite certain important people in the community.'

Later, Mr Ashoka telephoned Dr Whitecross and told him that the Parents' Committee had decided to hold a banquet in honour of the Director. Dr Whitecross replied that the Director usually visited schools to address pupils and teachers, but he felt certain that he would make an exception of Ashoka High.

When Friday evening arrived all the necessary precautions had been taken to ensure a trouble-free banquet. The Disciplinary Committee members, dressed in black suits and white shirts, stood guard outside the entrance door of the school hall and policemen patrolled the school and its precincts, carefully searching every corridor, examining every tree shadow, shining torches into hedge thickets.

Mr Ashoka, Dr Raj and the Parents' Committee members

stood in the foyer to welcome guests. Their wives were also present, dressed in shimmering saris of all colours. Everyone looked well-groomed and happy.

Inside the hall where the banquet was to take place waiters in black livery and waitresses in magenta uniforms moved about. A large quantity of flowers had been ordered for the occasion — even the foyer looked like a nursery — and these were being arranged in vases and placed on the tables. Three garlands, for the inspector, his wife and the Director, made of marigolds, carnations and chrysanthemums, were prominently displayed on the stage.

Soon guests began arriving: first came principals of schools, very punctual, and they were followed by important and influential members of the community. Among them was Dr Zia. Mr Ashoka had asked him to be one of the speakers at the function and he had agreed, provided his speech was recorded on tape. Mr Ashoka had readily conceded to his wish as he had already arranged to have all the speeches taped. Dr Zia had his ten-page speech 'in powerful English' (his own descriptive phrase) ready in his pocket. He was an inveterate speech-maker — his many speeches on casette tapes were on sale in stationery stores — and a member of every sort of organisation, from sports clubs that barely survived a season to political bodies, both anti-government and pro-government (he justified his position on the latter by saying that if he did not get on, scoundrels would). Then came several lawyers and more doctors: men who felt that life was not worth living without a Mercedes Benz and a spiralling bank balance. Then came several wealthy merchants, their bodies either bloated and warped, or skeletal and warped, by gluttony or asceticism; they were followed by several important sports personalities, men who were in control of sports organisations but had never played any sport in their lives.

When the Director's black Cadillac came to a halt in front of the school gate Mr Saeed and three other Disciplinary Committee members who had stationed themselves there since early evening went to the car and opened all the doors. Dr Whitecross and his wife emerged first and then the Director: a good-looking, tall, smiling man. Dr Whitecross introduced the teachers to his wife and the Director. Then everyone went towards the school hall.

The visitors were welcomed in the foyer by Mr Ashoka and his wife; they were then introduced to all the members of the Parents' Committee and their wives. They entered the hall and everyone stood up to welcome them.

Mr Ashoka led the way to the stage where the honoured guests were to be seated while speeches were delivered. Mrs Ashoka sat beside Mrs Whitecross. Mr Ashoka was master of ceremonies. Dr Raj was asked to be on the stage as well, but declined as he expected an emergency call from one of his patients; however, he would come on to the stage briefly to welcome the guests. Mr Ashoka then asked Dr Zia to join them on the stage and he readily agreed.

Mr Ashoka began by calling on Dr Raj to address the guests. He mounted the stage, extended a welcome to the guests of honour and all the others who were present, wished everyone a pleasant evening, and returned to his seat. Dr Zia came next. His speech, a blend of rhetoric and absurd bombast about 'august and noble personages and occasions blazing forever on the enigmatic conscience and residual psychology of the human race', left the waiters and waitresses wondering if the guests had come to a banquet of words. When he had finished Mr Ashoka

135

called upon a sports personality who had sent a note to him for permission to speak. He was a huge, obese man who leaned with both his hands on the lectern and spoke of his pet thesis that 'no man was truly educated who did not take an interest in some form of sport, even playing marbles.' He made several quips of a like kind, and the guests began to feel convivial after the copious medicinal dose of Dr Zia.

The next speaker was Dr Whitecross. 'Since I was appointed chief inspector,' he began, 'I have come to know the Indian pupil even better than the Indian parent does, if I may be allowed to say so. Under the influence of western civilisation the Indian pupil is among the most diligent, industrious and clever in the world. He is also the most obedient, respectful and law-abiding in the world. In fact I can confidently say . . . . '

After the inspector, Mr Ashoka addressed the gathering: 'It is a universally accepted fact that those persons who are responsible for the control of education shape the destinies of nations. A world at peace or a world at war is determined by what takes place in the classroom . . . . '

Finally, the Director gave his speech, of which the cardinal part was: 'I have great regard for the Indian race whose presence in this country is a lesson to those bent on creating disharmony. The Indian race has shown us what good manners, humility and, above all, what discipline means in creating racial harmony in this great country. It is because Indians — and I can say without hesitation that I know them as few Europeans know them — have decided to jealously guard their racial and cultural identities that they have made such great strides in the educational world. We have one of the world's great universities in Durban, the Indian University of Westville, where you can find the best professors and lecturers in the southern hemisphere.'

The Director was warmly applauded for his speech. Mr Ashoka then stood up from his chair and, taking a garland, approached the Director and placed it round his neck. He also garlanded Dr Whitecross, and Mrs Ashoka claimed the privilege of garlanding the inspector's wife. A photographer standing below the stage, used his flash repeatedly.

At this moment the rear door of the hall opened and ten pupils dressed in the uniforms of the various schools in Lenasia entered, carrying a garland in each hand. They marched in single file towards the front and climbed the steps that led to the stage. Everyone — except Mr Ashoka — applauded them, thinking that they were part of the evening's programme to honour the guests. One of the pupils, a boy, turned to the audience and addressed them in a rehearsed declamatory voice:

'Ladies and gentlemen, we have come with garlands to honour famous men and women; we honour them for their physical presence at this august gathering which, without them, would be left benighted; for their sublime intellects which stretch to the furthest galaxies of the universe in search of truth; for their learning which has enriched mankind's treasury of knowledge; for their wisdom which has guided legions of pupils to seek the wisdom which is their prerogative to bestow; above all, for the inalienable power and glory that is their crown and meed.'

There was loud applause. The Director was the first to be garlanded, then all the others stood up to accept theirs. The pupils, one after the other, put the garlands over the heads of the dignitaries who smiled benevolently — except Mr Ashoka whose face was like granite, dark, solemn,

Pharaoh-like. The pupils left the stage, marched through the hall in the same way they had entered, only pausing for a moment at the entrance door to thank the police who had been stationed there to keep out intruders.

On the stage, a constellation of dignitaries seemed to be submerged in a sea of fragrant flowers. They were applauded and photographed.

CHAPTER NINETEEN

Soon there began at Ashoka High School what many pupils in after years referred to as the time of 'The Reign of Terror'. The Disciplinary Committee members, instructed by the principal, took collective action against pupils who breached school regulations. Eight men armed themselves with canes and one of them flourished a pair of scissors as well. They started with the junior pupils first. They would knock at a door, enter a classroom and begin by inspecting the uniforms of pupils. (Many pupils, with the support of their parents, had refused to buy the new uniforms and the large quantity of unsold stock was beginning to vex Mr Ashoka; soon he would have to meet the manufacturer's bill.) All pupils not wearing the new uniforms were caned. Then came the turn of the pupils with long hair. The Disciplinary Committee barber used his scissors as inexpertly as possible. Then it was the turn of the girls who were wearing long pants and had not plaited their hair. They were given several strokes with the cane on their hands. By the time the Disciplinary Committee left a room, many pupils were whimpering.

When they reached Zenobia's room she was busy discussing a short story from Olive Schreiner's volume, *Dream Life and Real Life*. Mr Saeed asked for permission to enter. Zenobia saw the men armed with canes. She went to the doorway and asked Mr Saeed why they had come. He told her.

'I am afraid I cannot allow you in,' she said firmly.

'We have been instructed by the principal,' Mr Adam, the senior mathematics teacher said.

'You cannot come in,' Zenobia replied.

'We have to carry out our duties,' Mr Saeed insisted.

'You cannot come in,' Zenobia repeated, feeling a little annoyed.

The Disciplinary Committee members looked at each other. They were in a quandary. The pupils were looking at them. If they went away their authority would be diminished; if they entered without Zenobia's consent they might provoke an unpleasant incident with serious repercussions. Suddenly they walked away, as though impelled by their collective will.

During lunch break Zenobia spoke to the English teachers and she had no difficulty in persuading them to take a strong stand against the Disciplinary Committee. 'Violence and education cannot go together,' she said. 'These teachers, together with Mr Ashoka, have succumbed to the system.'

After school Zenobia was summoned to the office. She found the Disciplinary Committee there. Mr Ashoka said to her, 'You have, by not permitting the Disciplinary Committee to carry out its duties, disobeyed my instructions.'

'Yes,' she said calmly.

'Why?'

'I shall not permit any pupil to be beaten in my presence.'

'This is insubordination. I shall call the inspector.'

'Call whoever you want to, Mr Ashoka. You have become the image of your herrenvolk masters. You may know how to run a military camp, but not a school,' she said, turning and walking out of the office.

'Listen to her,' Mr Ashoka said to the Disciplinary Committee. 'You all heard what she said. She won't get away with this.'

The next day the news of the opposition by the English teachers spread through the school and several other teachers joined them. A rash of slogans appeared on blackboards: 'Gestapo get out!'; 'Ashoka's S.S. men have uniform minds!'; 'This school is now a military camp!' When Mr Ashoka came to hear of the growing opposition – his wounded dignity magnified the crisis – he called an assembly and threatened the pupils with expulsion if they failed to obey school regulations and objected to the function of the Disciplinary Committee.

'I want to see who will stop this committee from discharging its duties,' he challenged.

But after assembly the rebellion spread to all teachers not on the Disciplinary Committee. The Committee was paralysed. Mr Saeed went to Mr Ashoka to report the matter and asked him to call a staff meeting to restore authority. Mr Ashoka declined, fearing that he would be giving the defiant teachers an opportunity to attack him.

'I shall call the inspector to deal with them,' he said. 'In the meantime please suspend your activity.'

For the rest of the school day Mr Ashoka sat beside the intercommunication system listening in to teachers and hoping to catch some of them instigating the pupils to rebel. Instead he heard the following piece of conversation among pupils in a classroom where no teacher was present:

'Mr Ashoka has become power-mad.'

'He will end up in the asylum.'

'He should take some teachers with him to keep him company.'

'I can see Mr. Saeed goose-stepping through corridors.'

'Looking for Mr Adam without his fig leaf!'

Everyone laughed boisterously.

That evening *The Star* carried a brief article on the controversy at Ashoka High School. It gave the views of some anonymous pupils and teachers and a comment by Zenobia. 'Education and force,' she said, 'cannot go together. When eight men with canes enter a classroom to punish pupils for minor offences, they are no longer teachers but sadists. The psychological damage to the young can be considerable, especially to those who have come to high school this year.' The report stated that the principal of the school refused to speak to the press on the ground that 'the matter was internal', while the chairman of the Parents' Committee, Dr Raj, had refused to comment until he had received all the facts.

Early next morning Dr Whitecross arrived. 'I have read the report in the paper,' he said gravely, sitting down on a chair.

'The whole matter has been blown up by the gutter press,' Mr Ashoka said, pouring the tea that the secretary had brought. 'You know I set up the Disciplinary Committee to help me run the school more efficiently.'

'Did you record what happened yesterday in your log book?'

'Yes.'

'There is the possibility that the Department may make enquiries now that the matter has reached the press. May I have a look at the log book.'

Mr Ashoka gave the inspector the log book. He read the entry and then added his signature to Mr Ashoka's at the end.

'I don't know if the Department will want to pursue the matter,' Dr Whitecross said, 'but for the moment I think you should allow the Disciplinary Committee to become dormant. You and the vice-principal should personally deal with all cases of indiscipline among pupils.'

'I have the right to delegate my powers . . . . '

'Of course, but let things settle down. We must be patient . . . give them more rope.'

Mr Ashoka gave in reluctantly. His authority was being eroded and he did not feel happy. If the inspector went on in this indecisive way a time might come when he, the principal, was a prisoner of the staff and the pupils.

As Mr Ashoka accompanied Dr Whitecross to his car he said, 'Thank you for coming. Sometimes our work can be so trying.'

'Don't worry,' the inspector comforted him, 'I shall always stand by you. The Department will never abandon its officers.'

To add to Mr Ashoka's agony, *The Teachers' Chronicle* appeared after a few days. The activities of the Disciplinary Committee at Ashoka High School were condemned in the editorial written by Zenobia: 'Learning in an educational

143

humiliated

institution cannot take place in an atmosphere of brutality. The headmaster of the school, by establishing this committee, brought the methods of the police camp and military barracks to an institution where teachers are involved in the civilised business of educating children. Learning can only take place where there is freedom of thought, understanding, patience, dignity and love. The methods of the tyrant and the dictator must be kept out of the school.'

The editorial bit deeply into Mr Ashoka and he remained most of the time in his office, issuing instructions to teachers and pupils over the intercommunication system – at least, he consoled himself, one instrument of power remained in his hands. While he was master of it he could still exercise his authority.

And then one morning he came to school to find the system sabotaged – the speakers in all the classrooms were broken and the wires ripped out. He telephoned Dr Raj and told him to summon his committee immediately as something serious had occurred at school.

They came – the police also came at the same time – and examined the damage.

'This is not a case of vandalism,' he told the Parents' Committee as they sat down in his office to discuss the matter, 'but a deliberate attempt by a small group of teachers to destroy this school.'

'We will have to wait for the police report,' Dr Raj said cautiously.

'It will be appreciated that the system has to be repaired immediately,' Mr Ashoka went on. 'It is an invaluable educational aid and the school cannot be without it for long. But, gentlemen, there is another important matter I want you to attend to. Parents have not been co-operating in purchasing the new uniforms for their children. In fact not wearing the school uniform is a serious breach of school regulations. Pupils who do not wear uniforms become obstreperous and very soon get up to mischief and refuse to attend to their studies. I have had many complaints from my teachers. There is a large stock of uniforms in the store room and this must be cleared. The manufacturers cannot wait forever for payment. Please attend to the matter.'

Dr Raj replied that as a great deal of money would be needed to pay for repairs to the intercommunication system and the uniforms, his committee would have to call a meeting of all the parents to consider the matter.

'I can't wait for a parents' meeting,' Mr Ashoka said, getting angry.

'If we spend money on repairs we might find ourselves in trouble at the annual general meeting. In any case some of us were not in agreement when the intercommunication sytem was purchased . . . . '

'Am I then to blame for the vandalism? You are becoming insolent. It's the pupils, and the parents who have failed to teach them respect for educational property. Gentlemen, please carry out the function for which you were appointed. Thank you very much for coming.'

After the Committee had left, Mr Ashoka fumed. Who were they to accuse him of having insisted on purchasing the system against their better judgement? That doctor was merely a parasite, battening on the sick, dispensing pain-killing tablets and antibiotics indiscriminately for every illness. He would inform the Director of Education who would dismiss the entire Committee and appoint another to take its place.

CHAPTER TWENTY

For Mr Ashoka the collapse of the Disciplinary Committee took on the proportions of an intolerable personal humiliation. That body had been his own creation, representing his power and authority; his relationship to it equivalent to that of an artist to his work. That the body should have collapsed because it could not face the opposition of a single woman intensified the humiliation. He had tolerated Zenobia's opposition in his office and at meetings because professional formality had always acted as a shield. Now his creation was shattered. Zenobia had also — in his paranoia he had come to believe this — ejected him from her home. Feeling bitterly violated, he would never rest until he had damaged Zenobia's teaching career irretrievably. Night after night he sat brooding in his study, reading through the Education Act, and searching within its bureaucratic framework for the draconian clauses that would end her career. But first he had to devise the trap which would catch her in an act of insubordination.

She had been lucky to escape when she refused to comply with his order to celebrate Republic Day because of the political implications of her act. If he could capture her on legitimate educational grounds the Department would have no option but to charge her with insubordination and lead her to the mangle: the official enquiry. He remembered . . . two years ago the Department had issued a circular ordering all teachers to write a Daily Forecast of lessons, but his predecessor, in keeping with his laxity, had not enforced the order. He had considered the Daily Forecast as 'suitable for clerks, not teachers.' Now he, Mr Ashoka, would enforce it. If Zenobia refused to comply, and he believed she would, as defiance of his authority had become her stock reaction, he would have little difficulty in bringing her professional career to an end.

It was a simple instruction that went out to teachers one morning: 'You are hereby instructed to write a Daily Forecast of lessons in terms of the provisions of the circular R.A. 29. The Daily Forecast forms shall be issued to all teachers and these should be submitted to me personally every morning before the commencement of lessons. Circular R.A. 29 is attached herewith for your perusal and attention.'

When Mr Ashoka examined the Daily Forecast forms the next morning (essentially the Daily Forecast was a synopsis of lessons to be delivered during the nine periods each day, an elaboration of the daily time-table) and did not see the forms of the English teachers, he felt over-joyed. He knew that his triumph over Zenobia was now inevitable. If the other teachers wished to accompany her to the mangle he would not prevent them. He summoned them to his office and spoke bluntly.

'You refuse to comply with my instruction?'

'Yes. It is not possible to teach English according to an inflexible prescription.'

'I am not interested in your reason or reasons. Will all of you sign this statement please.'

In anticipation of their refusal, he had asked the secretary to prepare the following statement on separate sheets of paper: 'I hereby categorically refuse to comply with the Principal's order regarding the Daily Forecast.'

Each teacher signed the statement.

'This is a serious matter,' Mr Ashoka warned them. 'I hope you realise the serious consequences that can result from your defiance of my authority.'

Immediately the teachers left the office, a jubilant Mr Ashoka telephoned Dr Whitecross. He informed him of what had happened and concluded by saying that if the Department took no action against the teachers he would no longer be in a position of authority and he would 'have to think seriously of resigning.'

Dr Whitecross said he would come over to the school immediately. When he arrived Mr Ashoka went out to the gate to meet him. In his office he handed to him a copy of his instruction to all teachers, and the signed statements.

'There is a problem,' Dr Whitecross said reflectively.

'What problem? They have flouted my instruction and must be charged with insubordination by the Department. The matter is a clear-cut one this time. If nothing is done I might as well resign. The Department can find someone else to handle disrespectful teachers.'

'I understand your feelings,' Dr Whitecross said, 'but you will appreciate that to charge six teachers with misconduct at an official enquiry that will take place in the chief magistrate's court could lead to difficulties. I think you should submit a report on the lady only and leave the others out.'

'And what will happen if they present themselves at the enquiry and give evidence that they too refused to obey my instruction?'

'Their evidence will be irrelevant to the charge against the lady. We will say that she is the instigator, the ring-leader. Both of us will give evidence to that effect.'

'Thank you,' Mr Ashoka said.

'We have given her enough rope,' the inspector said. 'I think it is now time for us to hang her.'

Mr Ashoka laughed.

'Make your report to the Director and leave the rest to me,' the inspector assured him.

After a week Mr Ashoka received the following letter from the Director of Education to give to Zenobia:

You, Zenobia Hansa, occupying on a whole-time basis a post included in the establishment of the Ashoka High School, are hereby charged in terms of the provisions of sections 15, 16 and 17 of the Education Act (Act No 61 of 19 -) with misconduct as defined in section 16 (b) and section 16(c) of the said Act in that you attempted to defeat the ends of the State by disobeying, disregarding or making wilful default in carrying out a lawful order given to you by your superior in relation to the Daily Forecast as set out in the Departmental circular R.A. 29. Furthermore, you are hereby instructed in terms of section 17(3) of the aforementioned Act to transmit or deliver to the Director of Education, within 21 days of the

149

date of this letter, a written admission or denial of the charge and, if you so desire, a written explanation of the misconduct with which you are charged. Should you deny the charge of misconduct against you, you shall be informed in due course of the time, date and place of enquiry.

After reading the letter, Mr Ashoka decided that it would be his pleasure to hand it to Zenobia personally instead of sending his secretary with it. He put it into an official envelope and with jaunty steps went to Zenobia's room, but found it empty. He looked at the time-table on the wall and saw that she had a poetry lesson. Where could she be? Perhaps she had taken the pupils to the library. He hurried there and looked through the window. The librarian was alone. Perhaps she had taken the pupils to the playground for a poetry lesson out of doors. She did that occasionally. He went towards the playground and saw her sitting under a tree, surrounded by pupils. He hurried towards her. She saw him approaching with a letter in his hand, outstretched prematurely. He came up, greeted the pupils and said to her, 'I have an official letter for you from the Director of Education.'

The pupils made way for him and he handed Zenobia the letter. He smiled at her. Then he turned and walked away.

Zenobia took the letter and put it into her handbag. She had been discussing Liu Tzu-hui's 'Autumn Moonlight' with the pupils before Mr Ashoka's arrival. She went on, though she knew that the letter spelt some complication over the Daily Forecast.

Mr Ashoka looked back twice to see if she would open the letter, but her eyes were upon the children, speaking to them, trying to awaken them:

> *The flying brightness shimmers through the grove,*
> *And, mirrored on the pine-ringed pool,*
> *Makes her dream-waters beautiful.*

Later, in the staff room, during the tea-break, Zenobia read the letter. Although surprised that the Department would want to make a public issue over a triviality such as the Daily Forecast, she was not shocked. The bureaucratic mind could not act in any other way. Zenobia showed the letter to the English teachers and soon everyone wanted to know the contents. One of the teachers then read it aloud. They listened and were stunned, even the teachers who had served on the defunct Disciplinary Committee. They felt threatened; morally rather than professionally. What could they say to Zenobia? The bureaucratic, authoritarian thrust of the letter froze them into silence.

That afternoon, when she reached home, she read the letter again and had an uncanny feeling that Mr Ashoka would gain his victory and that she would not see the year out at the school.

When her husband came home in the evening she showed him the letter.

'It seems that your days at the school are nearing an end,' Kamar said. 'The letter speaks of a "lawful order". Any order coming from one of higher authority is lawful. Its reasonableness is not in question. I will check tomorrow in the Education Act. Anyway, we will have to put up a fight.' He put his arms around her shoulders to comfort her.

The prospect of her teaching career coming to an end filled Zenobia with sadness; the close relationship she had woven with her pupils would be severed. She had enhanced her own sensibilities by attempting to cultivate the sensibilities of her pupils; she had done so by transcending the threshold of prescriptive academic work. That night she came to feel, as intimately as her entire being could feel it, the enormous power of those who knew no happiness nor wished others to possess it. Unable to sleep, she went to the bedroom of her children and sat down beside them as they slumbered peacefully.

CHAPTER TWENTY-ONE

Kamar, with an artist's brush in his hand, was sitting on a stool in front of a canvas on an easel under an acacia tree. He was a symmetrically-proportioned man with black hair receding from a tan forehead; his nose was almost classically Grecian in its sculpted look; his eyes, beneath the gentle curve of his elegant eyebrows, were rusty brown. He was trying to blend on a palette an exact shade of green pigment that would capture the abundant verdant life of a mass of reeds growing along the banks of a stream a hundred feet below him. Beyond the stream was a parkland of acacias, cypresses and conifers. Zenobia and the children, the two young ones, Masood and Zeenat, could be seen among the trees gathering wild flowers. Every now and then the children would run up to their mother with cries of joy, finding an unusually attractive flower amid the grass or seeing a colourful dappled butter-fly. Kamar, looking up from the palette for a moment, saw his wife and children move further away and disappear among a clump of trees.

Zenobia had started the painting before she had taken the children across the stream for a ramble. Kamar was now completing it. He looked at the canvas before him, and slowly, delicately, painted the green swords of the reeds. Then he looked at the reeds along the stream and saw a swarm of yellow birds disappear into them and set them astir with their chirping.

Kamar was filled with a deep sense of tranquillity, which was enhanced by the satisfaction that he had recently successfully concluded a lengthy defence of some twenty school pupils who had been charged with arson, malicious damage to state property, conspiracy to over-throw the state, instigating others to revolt and intent to flee the country illegally in order to take up arms.

The weavers among the reeds rose suddenly in a swarm as though they had received a telepathic order from beyond the skies, traced a perfect arc and came flying towards the acacia under which Kamar was seated. They passed overhead. The reeds were still now, though Kamar could hear silence breeding in the dense mass. And then he heard, as though the silence had given birth to it, the single, sharp, flute-like call of a bird.

Kamar went on painting. Then he saw Zenobia emerging from a clump of trees and coming towards him. The children did not follow her. She came slowly, stopping for a moment to pick a wild flower. She was dressed in a pastel-pink blouse and a cerise skirt. A matching silk scarf patterned with bouquets of tiny roses was tied around her neck. A string of rose quartz beads decorated her bosom. When she reached the stream she took off her red shoes and then stepped on a flat stone, one of a bridge-like series in the stream. She waved to her husband to come. Kamar put his palette and brushes down and went towards her.

Zenobia stopped in the middle of the stream. In her hand was the blue daisy-like flower she had picked. She looked at her foreshortened form in the stream's mirror; vari-coloured pebbles lay in the shallow water. With a feeling of joyful trepidation she put her right foot into the water and felt its effervescent coolness reach above her ankle. She put her other foot in. Her husband stood on the bank looking at her.

'It's cool and lovely,' she said. 'Take off your sandals and come in.'

'Where are the children?' he asked.

'They are playing with pine cones.'

Kamar stepped into the water and went towards her. When he reached her she used the flower in her hand as a wand, tracing an invisible pattern on his forehead, cheeks and chin; then she flung her arms around him and kissed him tenderly, lovingly. The flower fell into the stream, its blue face upturned, and pausing for a moment beside a stone to say farewell, drifted away.

Husband and wife stood in the languidly flowing stream; the reeds rustled coyly around them; petal-soft clouds floated in a sky of unblemished blue. A swarm of weavers came and settled nearby in the reeds for a moment, then rose in alarm as the children came running down towards their parents standing in the stream, their voices ringing with joy, their hands laden with flowers.

Kamar lifted Zenobia in his arms, carried her across and put her down on the grass. Then he crossed the stream to the opposite bank where the children were standing; he let them climb on to his shoulders and then walked across the bridge of stones, stopping at intervals to allow the children to see themselves in the water's mirror.

Zenobia lay in the fragrant grass, looking up at the sky. Kamar and the children came to where she lay. Kamar took a few flowers from the children and playfully let them fall on her face. This provided a signal for the children to pelt their mother with flowers, which they did with joy and laughter.

A swarm of weavers winged overhead, but did not settle among the reeds.

CHAPTER TWENTY-TWO

It was a bright morning in early spring when Zenobia rose to face the enquiry in the chief magistrate's court. The Department had been careful to hold the enquiry on a school day so that neither teachers nor pupils could attend. However, when Zenobia reached the court with her husband and children she was met by a number of pupils who had decided to brave Mr Ashoka's anger by not attending school. Several newspaper reporters were also present; in fact a morning newspaper carried Zenobia's photograph and gave a brief account of the charge she was facing. Zenobia, surrounded by her family, pupils and friends, stood in the corridor in front of the court room. Mr Ashoka stood a little distance away. He was alone. Dr Whitecross approached him and shook his hand. The two men spoke to each other, with strained faces. Although the public prosecutor, during his interviews with the two men, had assured them that Zenobia would be found guilty, they did not feel happy. They would find themselves in the witness box and be subject to cross-examination by the lawyer, and this was something they did not look foward to, as it would involve a reduction of their dignities. While Mr Ashoka was speaking to Dr Whitecross, he saw Dr Raj and members of the Parents' Committee pass by without as much as looking at him. They went towards Zenobia and shook her hand. Then came Prince Yusuf and the women: Eleanor, Anne-Marie, Cordell, Charmaine. Even Eleanor's servant Phyllis was there. Mr Ashoka felt a sudden constriction within him. They were elegantly dressed and walked past as though they were at a fair. As Eleanor passed by, she looked haughtily at him and flicked the ash at the tip of the cigarette in its mother-of-pearl holder. They went on to join Zenobia.

'Who are they?' Dr Whitecross asked.

'I don't know,' Mr Ashoka replied, feeling a tightening in his throat. He realised that he had been foolish to alienate Prince Yusuf; he could have had his support, and that of the ladies, now.

Zenobia, having accepted the possibility that her teaching career would end soon, looked serene in a golden sari. Her husband was going to defend her and she felt a resurgence of the joy that had filled her on her wedding day, when her consciousness had been deluged by his presence.

The courtroom contained a great deal of brown timber, from the seats for the spectators to the platform on which was placed the magistrate's seat. The public prosecutor sat at a table below the magistrate and beside him, one of his clerks. Zenobia sat in the gallery with the spectators. Several orderlies entered the room and took up positions at various strategic places, near the doors, the dock, and the trap-door enclosure from which criminal suspects who were kept in the cells under the court building were brought up during trials. As soon as the magistrate entered, accompanied by an assessor who had been appointed by the Department, an orderly barked and everyone rose.

The magistrate was a tall man with white hair and a small white beard. The assessor, who was an inspector of education in Durban, was a small dark austere-looking man who gave one the impression that at some stage in his educational career his face had suffered a seizure and was no longer capable of human expression.

The prosecutor, who seemed to be a replica of the court orderlies who were all big-boned with their hair cut very short, rose from his chair, went towards the magistrate and handed him the charge sheet. The magistrate then began the proceedings.

'Will the accused by the name of Mrs Zenobia Hansa please take her position in the witness box.'

Zenobia rose from her seat, walked to the front of the courtroom, climbed three steps and entered the witness box. She took the oath and the prosecutor began with formalities: he asked her if she was the person named in the charge sheet, if she was employed by the Education Department, if she was a teacher at the Ashoka High School in Lenasia. He then read the charge against her: 'In terms of sections 15, 16 and 17 of the Education Act of 19-, Zenobia Hansa is charged with misconduct in attempting to defeat the ends of the State by refusing to comply with a lawful order given to her by her superior in relation to the Daily Forecast of lessons, and that the court find her guilty of misconduct as defined in the said Act under section 16(b) which reads: "he does or causes or permits to be done or connives at anything which is prejudicial to

159

the administration, discipline or efficiency of any department, office or institution of the State" and section 16(c) which reads: "he disobeys, disregards or makes wilful default in carrying out a lawful order given to him by a person having authority to give it, or by word or conduct displays insubordination".' The prosecutor read 'Annexure A', the Department's circular R.A. 29 relating to the Daily Forecast; he read 'Annexure B', the circular issued by Mr Ashoka to teachers to write the Daily Forecast; he read 'Annexure C', the signed statement by Zenobia that she refused to comply with the headmaster's order. He then handed the documents to the magistrate and addressed the court briefly.

'Your worship, as the facts of the case are not in dispute, I submit that the court find the accused guilty of misconduct as defined in the Education Act.'

He sat down and the magistrate asked Zenobia if she had anything to say about the documents handed in to the court and she said no. The magistrate then asked the assessor if he had anything to say, but he only moved his head slowly to the left and to the right.

Kamar then prepared to cross examine Mr Ashoka who climbed into the witness box. An orderly adjusted the microphone speaker for him.

'Mr Ashoka,' Kamar began, 'you are, I believe, a very learned man. I understand you have three degrees. Is that correct?'

'Yes, I have a Bachelor of Arts degree, an Honours Bachelor of Arts Degree and a Bachelor of Education degree.'

'That is very commendable indeed. Now before me on my table are various books by well-known educationists. I am sure you have read them.'

Kamar lifted the books and read the various titles and the names of the authors.

'Yes,' Mr Ashoka admitted, though he had never read them as they had been published recently.

'Now, having glanced at these books there seems to me to be a consensus among the educationists that the emphasis on uniformity at schools is a form of tyranny, which can seriously affect the quality of teaching, as well as having very serious consequences on the mental development of pupils. Do you agree?'

Mr Ashoka found himself in a dilemma: if he disagreed and said that he considered discipline to be of paramount importance, then the lawyer might refer to the content of some of the books and he might find himself embarrassed, having already claimed that he had read the books; on the other hand if he agreed with the authors there was the danger of being trapped in a contradiction. He decided to take the second course as being less of a threat to his dignity.

'Yes, I agree.'

'Don't you think, Mr Ashoka, that the Daily Forecast is an instrument that furthers the tyranny of uniformity at school?'

The prosecutor immediately objected on a point of order.

'Your worship, I submit that the question is irrelevant. The question is whether the teacher received a lawful instruction or not and whether she complied or refused to comply with it.'

The magistrate asked Kamar to proceed.

'Mr Ashoka, will you now answer my question.'

'The Daily Forecast is an instrument that promotes efficient teaching.'

'In what way?'

'The teacher consults the Daily Forecast and knows what to teach.'

'But I am made to understand that the Daily Forecast must be handed to you before school begins, and that would seem to suggest that it is for your benefit.'

Mr Ashoka said nothing further.

'Now, to go on, can you tell me why the previous headmaster of the school did not ask the teachers to write a Daily Forecast?'

'It lay within his discretion.'

'Do I understand that your order to write it also lay within your discretion?'

'Yes.'

'Did you have any reason when you asked the teachers to write it?'

'I felt that, although the Daily Forecast was not compulsory, the Department must have considered it of educational value to recommend it.'

'In other words you gave it no thought of your own?'

'I did.'

'Did you tell the teachers what you thought to be the merits of it?'

'No.'

'And why didn't you?'

'I didn't think it was necessary.'

'Because you wished to dragoon the teachers? You wanted to show them your authority?'

The prosecutor objected again.

'Your worship, I fail to see the relevance of the learned

advocate's questions. Motives are not at issue here.'

The magistrate asked Kamar to continue.

'Mr Ashoka, can you explain why you waited to introduce the Daily Forecast, which you consider to be of great educational value, at this time of the year and not at the beginning?'

'I wanted the school to run smoothly before introducing it.'

'In other words you did not consider it very important.'

'I considered it to be very important, but there were other more important organisational matters to attend to.'

'Such as changing the name of the school to the Ashoka High School?'

'The Parents' Committee changed the name.'

'Didn't you suggest it to them?'

'No.'

'I have a copy of the minutes of the Parents' Committee meeting. I shall read the relevant extract to you.'

The lawyer read the extract.

'Surely, if you wished to honour the emperor, the name of the school should have been the Emperor Ashoka High School?'

Mr Ashoka remained silent.

'You wanted to perpetuate your own name, is that not true?'

'That is not true.'

'Now, Mr Ashoka, I want to suggest to you that because you could not tolerate teachers whose views on education differed from your own, that you decided to force them to write the Daily Forecast?'

'That was not my intention. I looked at it purely from an educational point of view.'

The prosecutor rose to object: 'Your worship, what has all this to do with an order that was given and disobeyed?'

'Your worship, I wish to prove mala fides on the head-master's part.'

The magistrate allowed Kamar to continue.

'Now, I have been informed that all the English teachers refused to write the Daily Forecast. Is that correct?'

'Yes.'

'And these happened to be the same teachers who refused to attend the flag-raising ceremony on Republic Day?'

'Yes.'

'Then why did you inform the Department that only one teacher refused to obey your order regarding the Daily Forecast?'

'I regarded Zenobia Hansa as the ringleader, the instigator.'

'If you reported her only, and did not mention the names of the other teachers, how can the court consider her as a ringleader? You are asking us to accept the fact of a conspiracy without showing us the conspirators. Please tell the court why you reported her only?'

Mr Ashoka remained silent.

'To go on. Have the English teachers at the school, after having learnt that Zenobia Hansa was to be charged with misconduct, decided to write the Daily Forecast?'

'No.'

'And what are you going to do?'

'That is left to my discretion.'

'So there is a possibility that they may never be charged?'

'I won't say that. The Department has many ways of dealing with insubordination.'

'But you have not yet reported them to the Department. Do you intend to?'

'That is left to my discretion.'

'I see. Finally, can you tell me whether you consider Zenobia Hansa to be an efficient or an inefficient teacher?'

'I would say an efficient teacher.'

Kamar completed his cross-examination of Mr Ashoka. The magistrate asked the principal several minor questions and then asked the assessor if he had any questions to ask. He shook his head slowly.

Dr Whitecross was asked to enter the witness box. After the usual formalities, Kamar asked him if Mr Ashoka called him to the school when the English teachers failed to submit their Daily Forecasts.

'Yes.'

'Did he tell you that Zenobia Hansa was the ringleader and that he would report her only to the Department?'

'No.'

'So, you would say that the headmaster erred in reporting her only?'

'Yes.'

'Why do you think he suppressed the information about the others?'

'I don't know.'

'Do you think he acted from malevolence?'

'I am unable to comment.'

'When you discovered that only Zenobia Hansa was to be arraigned in court did you question Mr Ashoka on the propriety?'

'No.'

'Why not?'

'The principal knows his business best.'

'Even when you perceived that what he was doing was improper?'

The inspector did not respond.

'Dr Whitecross, can you tell the court the use of the Daily Forecast?'

'It informs the principal what lesson a teacher is busy with during a particular period.'

'Can the teacher change his mind and give another lesson?'

'He cannot. If he gives another lesson it would show that he does not know his work and disciplinary action can be taken against him.'

'Even if he feels that pupils do not understand what he is attempting to explain and decides to revise some previous work before continuing?'

'He cannot.'

'Assuming he is asked a question and decides to spend the entire period answering the question?'

'He cannot in terms of what he has set out to do.'

'I have no further questions.'

The magistrate was on the point of adjourning the hearing for a short intermission when a court messenger entered with a letter for Kamar. Kamar read the letter and said, 'Your worship, an important witness for the defence has arrived from Cape Town. He is the former headmaster of the school, Mr Mahara, now living in retirement. I ask for permission to question him now as he is leaving for India shortly and has to return home as soon as possible.'

The magistrate gave his consent and the messenger went out and returned with Mr Mahara. Kamar went up to him, shook his hand and asked him to enter the witness box.

Everyone looked at Mr Mahara, except Mr Ashoka; his

predecessor's appearance in court was as unexpected as that of a man long dead, a man whose memory had been erased from all records. A squall of fear came over him and he bowed his head and looked at his feet.

Mr Mahara was not a tall man. He looked much younger than his sixty-six years. His partly grey hair was thick and long, cascading around his ears and coat collar. His face was smooth and serene. There was something foreign about him, and also ancient: he seemed to belong to some legendary age and time when human beings lived in harmony.

'Mr Mahara,' Kamar said, 'can you tell the court why you did not ask the teachers to submit the Daily Forecast?'

'I saw nothing in it that could benefit anyone. It seemed to me an instrument of control that could inspire fear, and lead to strain and joyless teaching. When teachers are not free in a classroom, then there is the danger that they will no longer behave like sensitive beings capable of using their imaginations.'

'Thank you very much,' Kamar said. 'Is there anything else that you would like to add.'

'Yes. I believe that knowledge, though our age considers it primarily utilitarian, is of intrinsic worth, a good in itself, and everything should be done to make its acquisition a joy. In this way life is enhanced.'

Kamar then turned to the prosecutor and asked him if he wished to question Mr Mahara. He said no. Mr Mahara then took his leave, lifting his hand in the doorway to say farewell to everyone.

The magistrate adjourned the court for a short intermission. In the corridor everyone crowded around Zenobia while Mr Ashoka had only one person to talk to, the assessor. The magistrate, the prosecutor and the inspector had gone to a whites-only canteen in the court building for tea.

Prince Yusuf and his harem stood among the people around Zenobia, who looked very regal in her sari. While Mr Ashoka was talking to the assessor, Prince Yusuf and the ladies went towards them. They stopped in front of the two men and looked at them as though they were museum pieces. Mr Ashoka kept his eyes lowered but when he stole a momentary glance at them as they were about to move away, he saw Eleanor tilt her head disdainfully upwards at him. Prince Yusuf and the ladies walked away and rejoined Zenobia.

When the court re-assembled Zenobia was called into the witness box by her counsel and asked to give her view of education. She succinctly outlined her approach to teaching and the atmosphere in which it could flourish. She ended by saying, 'I felt that the Daily Forecast was a serious invasion of a teacher's liberty; and I also felt that by accepting an authoritarian procedure I would, as time went on, begin to compromise with authoritarianism and subtly influence the pupils as well.'

Her view of education was not appreciated by the prosecutor, who informed the magistrate that he wished to ask her a few questions. The magistrate consented.

'Do you consider discipline important at school or not?'

'That depends on what you mean by discipline.'

'Carrying out an order shows discipline; not carrying it out is indiscipline.'

'I am afraid my view differs from yours. By discipline I understand rational, moral and cultural growth, not obedience for the sake of obedience.'

'What will you do when pupils do not listen to your instructions.'

'As a teacher I do not issue instructions. I learn to grow in mind and heart with the children.'

The prosecutor then summed up by saying that there was a clear case of insubordination, admitted by the teacher, and that the court could not fail to find her guilty. The counsel for the defence summed up by saying that his client had been placed in a situation which required her to betray her entire conception of education to satisfy a headmaster's irrational demand.

The court adjourned for half an hour, and when the magistrate returned with the assessor in tow, he gave his verdict:

'The court finds the accused, Mrs Zenobia Hansa, guilty of not obeying a lawful order in relation to the Daily Forecast of lessons given to her by her superior. However, the court also finds that the accused refused to comply with the order, not because of wilful insubordination, but because the order conflicted with her educational principles. The court also finds her to have been an efficient teacher.

'The findings of the court shall be referred to the Director of Education who shall, in terms of the provisions of the Education Act, decide on punishment.'

After the enquiry Mr Ashoka stood in the corridor alone for a few minutes; the assessor had left hurriedly to take the plane back to Durban and Dr Whitecross had walked away without saying a word to him. He saw Zenobia surrounded by all the spectators who had come to court. She was smiling as they shook her hand; pressmen took her photograph and asked her a few questions. There was an air of jubilation as though she had triumphed in the legal tussle.

A profound sense of doom came over him as he walked away.

170

CHAPTER TWENTY-THREE

After a week Mr Ashoka received the Director's letter to Zenobia dismissing her from the teaching profession 'on the grounds of misconduct as determined at the official enquiry'. He sat in his office and looked at the letter for a long while. He did not feel triumphant. He feared that Zenobia's dismissal might unleash public hate against him (he remembered his loneliness at the enquiry) and even lead undisciplined persons to attack him and his family. Why was the ultimate action taken against her when there were several options open to the Director? He could have had her transferred to another school or magnanimously given her a stringent warning. Perhaps if he telephoned Dr Whitecross and spoke to him he could have the decision changed. But he had not seen the inspector since the enquiry; perhaps he was keeping away because he felt ashamed at the evidence he had given in court, the lie. Yet Mr Ashoka had forgiven him; to be cross-examined is an unnerving experience.

He telephoned Dr Whitecross, told him of the letter and then read it to him.

'We gave her enough rope,' Dr Whitecross said, 'and now she has hanged herself. I am sure you are very happy at the result. You will now have discipline among your teachers.'

Mr Ashoka had not the courage to tell the inspector that he should approach the Director for a lesser punishment for Zenobia; and neither could he go to her and give her the letter. He sent for Mr Saeed and asked him to deliver it, after telling him of the contents.

'It will be my pleasure to give the letter to her,' Mr Saeed said. 'I believe trouble-makers must be weeded out.' Mr Saeed remembered the humiliation he had suffered when Zenobia had not permitted him to carry out his duties as leader of the Disciplinary Committee.

'You don't think the action is a bit drastic?' Mr Ashoka enquired.

'Not at all. I wish we had the power to hire and fire teachers. They would soon learn to jump at our commands.'

Zenobia's dismissal provoked the anger of many people in the community. All the newspapers carried the news and there was strong condemnation of Mr Ashoka and the Department. The Parents' Committee immediately summoned a meeting of all the parents to protest at her dismissal. Dr Raj telephoned Mr Ashoka and asked him to be present at the meeting.

'The matter is very serious,' he said. Mr Ashoka pointed out that as a mere principal he could not alter the Director's decision. 'The entire community is seriously perturbed by the issue,' Dr Raj went on.

'I am in full agreement that the community must do

172

something,' Mr Ashoka assured the doctor. 'The action taken by the Director is extreme, but it has nothing to do with me. If I were to come to the meeting people might think I am responsible.'

'But don't you think if you come and tell the people of your position and that you disagree with the drastic action taken by the Director, there would a better chance of getting Zenobia reinstated?'

'Dr Raj, please leave me out.'

'Perhaps we could even discuss the repair of the inter-communication system and the payment for the uniforms.'

'That can be done at some other time,' Mr Ashoka replied, putting the telephone back on its cradle. He knew that Dr Raj was trying to lure him to the meeting so that he could attack him in the presence of a large, emotionally aroused audience. Even the bait of the restoration of the intercommunication system and the payment for the uniforms — a second bill had recently come in — would not lead him there.

He looked at the control panel of the intercommunicat-ion system. He fingered the switches, one at a time. No green and red lights flickered. The system was dead. He felt a steel clamp closing within him.

The meeting, held in the Ramakrishna Hall, was an angry one. Dr Raj led the attack against Mr Ashoka, detailing the demands he had made on the Committee's financial resources, his maladminstration of the school, culminating in Zenobia's dismissal. Three resolutions were adopted at the meeting: the Parents' Committee would not hold itself responsible for repairs to the intercommunication system nor the payment for the new uniforms; an appeal would be made to the Director to reinstate Zenobia; should the appeal fail a petition calling for Mr Ashoka's dismissal would be circulated in the community. Among the people who volunteeered to obtain signatures in support of the petition was Prince Yusuf.

The next day, a report of the meeting appeared in the newspapers. Fortunately for Mr Ashoka it was a Sunday. He kept to his study most of the time — his wife had gone to visit a friend and he had generously allowed Deva to go to the sports field. In the silence of his study he felt himself locked in the epicentre of a cyclone, awaiting the moment when it would sweep through the city, hurtling him, with the debris, through streets, against office towers and apartment blocks.

On Monday he telephoned Dr Whitecross and asked him to come over to the school as he wished to tell him of the 'campaign of vilification certain individuals in the community had embarked upon.' The inspector said that he had much work to do, but Mr Ashoka could rest assured that the 'entire Department' would stand by him in any crisis.

'The newspapers are trying to sensationalise the whole issue and are presenting me as a villain,' Mr Ashoka complained.

'Oh, just ignore the gutter press. One day we shall have all these newspapers banned by the government.'

'In the meantime . . . . '

'Don't worry, Mr Ashoka. We have got rid of that troublesome witch. How long can the newspapers go on writing about her. Soon the public will get tired and she will be of news value no longer. She will be forgotten.'

Mr Ashoka found no comfort in the inspector's words.

During the evening, sitting in the study with Deva, who was trying to do his homework, Mr Ashoka confided in him.

'I am having a lot of trouble from some teachers, Deva.'

'Yes,' Deva answered indifferently, going over a geometrical construction with pencil and ruler as though it were a pattern that had to be traced. He worked methodically, joylessly at it. Mr Ashoka allowed him to go on.

Since the time his son had run away, he had become lenient towards him, often setting him no additional homework and even permitting him to play with friends and go to the cinema more than once a week. Deva, instead of being pleased at his father's relaxed hold on him, seemed to recede into sullenness. He sat there now, self-contained, his forehead contracted, oblivious of his father's presence.

CHAPTER TWENTY-FOUR

The anger of teachers in Lenasia over Zenobia's dismissal was soon exacerbated by an article written 'by the well-known educationists, Dr P. Whitecross and Mr D. Ashoka.' The article, entitled 'Differential Educational Criteria for the Twentieth Century', appeared in the Department's quarterly magazine *Pro Veritate*. Two of its paragraphs read:

'The caste system is the product of the great civilisation of India. It was established on sound practical, intellectual, social and moral principles, by the ancient Aryans who arrived on the sub-continent of India several millennia ago. It recognises the inherent natural differences among human races and forms the basis for an ordered society where every human being has his place. That human beings are different racially, socially, psychologically, ethnically is a truth that so-called humanists who wish to reduce humanity to an undifferentiated mass, a grey mass we may say, have attempted to deny. The ancient social architects of India enshrined the noble truth of differentiation among human beings in their holy books, the Gita and the Upanishads. The entire social fabric on the sub-continent of India was based on strict stratification: there were the priest-class Brahmins, the warrior-class Kshatriyas, the merchant-class Vaisyas, and the labourer-class Sudras. Differentiation was implemented in India long before the philosopher Plato could think of it.

'It should be evident to all clear-thinking teachers that the official policy of Differential Education as practised in South Africa follows closely the unique system evolved in India by its sages. Of course our policy is very much more sophisticated to suit modern times. Our policy is to allow all the various races of our country to develop to the maximum their own particular way of life as enshrined in their histories, cultures, languages — and not to impose the tyranny of uniformity that can only destroy the God-given individualities of the races of the world. The caste system stands for law and order. Differential Education also stands for law and order. The State policy of Separate Development is nothing other than the caste system developed to a very high degree by our political scientists. Differential Education, an aspect of that policy, is a unique twentieth century phenomenon conceived by the best intellects of this age.'

Incensed by the article, the reaction of teachers was swift. Even headmasters of other schools who had remained neutral over Zenobia's dismissal, condemned Mr Ashoka. A petition to summon a special general meeting of the Teachers' Association was circulated after Mr Ashoka had refused to call a meeting to discuss the article. One evening Mr Ashoka was handed the petition by the secretary.

177

'Who engineered this petition?' he asked angrily.

'That is irrelevant,' the secretary answered. 'I am calling the meeting.'

After the secretary had left Mr Ashoka fumed at the bad faith of the inspector who had not told him what he wished to do with the article on the caste system and Hindu philosophy he had written for him. And why had the man not claimed sole responsibility for the *Pro Veritate* article instead of involving him? Would the teachers ever believe him if he told them the truth? In fact some might ask him to repudiate it, which of course he could never do without bringing the wrath of the entire Department upon him. There was only one exit for him — resign the presidency of the Teachers' Association. Which he did, on the day of the meeting, by sending a letter to the secretary.

This meeting too, like that of the Parents' Committee, was an angry one. Mr Ashoka was strongly condemned for having written with Inspector Whitecross 'an article offensive to the teaching profession'. He was also condemned for having been instrumental in Zenobia's dismissal. A resolution was adopted calling on the Director of Education to reinstate Zenobia, and another one retaining her membership of the Association and her position as editor of *The Teachers' Chronicle*.

The newsletter soon appeared with the following editorial, entitled 'Authoritarianism and Education':

'Authoritarianism in educational institutions is a product of the political order in the country. An administrative hierarchy, operating within the confines of a claustral political system, is soon transformed into a body of functionaries and bureaucrats masquerading as education-ists. Power and authority is institutionalised by forms, rules and regulations. The aim of an authoritarian system of education is the obliteration of individuality in pupils and teachers and the achievement of robot-like uniformity by regimentation and conditioning. Authoritarianism has always been with us (in the prevailing political order it couldn't be otherwise) but in recent years with the introduction of Differential Education it has begun to display itself with increasing arrogance.

'A humane conception of education has certain ends in view which reach beyond the static absolutist world of authoritarians. By education is meant the mental development of the individual to his or her full potential; the acquisition of knowledge and culture; the cultivation of individual thought and opinion; the development of a critical intelligence that will engage in discussion, debate and argument not only about academic subjects that form part of the curriculum, but also existential realities and problems; the development of the capacity for abstract thought; the maturing of the range of human sensibilities, sensuous and sensual, intellectual, aesthetic, emotional, intuitive; the refinement of the perception of life values; the animation of the creative faculty where fusion of the imagination and the intellect gives birth to new structure and forms; and, finally, perhaps even the enhancement of the conceptions of the ideals of beauty, love, truth, liberty, happiness. In essence, humane education leads to the maturing and consummation of being.

'When education comes under the heel of authoritarianism it increasingly comes to mean memorising of facts and their reproduction during examinations. Teachers and lecturers become preachers, purveyors of dogma and infallible truth. Independent and original thought becomes dangerous heresy. Authoritarianism is out to exert control, and control can only be exercised over a herd or over automatons. Stereotyped behaviour is encouraged as being virtuous and meritorious; those who wish to be different are denigrated as "trouble-makers" or worse still "instigators" and "rebels". Perverted forms of differentiation are encouraged, those based on race and colour. Under authoritarianism the educational institution takes on the trappings of a military camp: there are inflexible rules and regulations; superiors must be obeyed; instructions and orders are always issued; there is the emphasis on superficial display and forms; the compulsory wearing of uniforms (and the obsessional hatred of long hair!); there is the cult-like devotion to athletics and sports; the pride in name and buildings; the exaggerated importance of examination results, and so on. In this sort of atmosphere teachers and lecturers who disagree are threatened, disciplined, transferred, or dismissed. Of those who remain, many are silenced by fear while others become obsessed with advancement and promotion (to join the hierarchy, gain power over others and maintain the status quo); pupils and students are pressured into submission (openly-elected representative bodies with their own constitutions are not permitted) and the ultimate result is a mass of automatons amenable to easy manipulation.'

CHAPTER TWENTY-FIVE

One morning Dr Whitecross arrived at the school unexpectedly. As soon as he entered the office Mr Ashoka noticed the astringent look on his face.

'Where is the flag?' Dr Whitecross asked.

'Flag, sir?'

'The sacred national flag of the country.'

'It is in the strong-room.'

'Please show it to me.'

Mr Ashoka took the keys, opened the steel door, went in and returned with the case in which the flag was kept. He put the case on the table.

'Open it,' Dr Whitecross commanded.

Mr Ashoka opened it. There was no flag but only the rope. 'It was there,' he said defensively.

'That's not true. It disappeared after the flag-raising ceremony.'

'I asked Mr Saeed to see to its safety,' Mr Ashoka recalled. 'It had been a day of trouble.'

'Did you not receive a confidential letter from the Department telling you not to raise the flag if you suspected trouble? Send for Mr Saeed.'

Mr Ashoka went to his secretary's room and asked her to call the vice-principal. He did not return to his office immediately, but stood there for a while looking at an abstract painting of a deformed goldfish in a glass bowl.

The inspector had arrived at the school after receiving a letter from Mr Saeed, which read in part: 'At the end of the school day I went to the assembly place but did not see our national flag. I made enquiries but no one could tell me what had happened to it. I placed the flag rope in its case and handed it to the secretary for safe-keeping. I did not tell Mr Ashoka that the flag was missing, as I knew that it was a gross dereliction of duty on his part to have raised the flag, when he knew that trouble was brewing over the ceremony among pupils and teachers. But my conscience and my loyalty to the Department have now compelled me to inform you of what happened.'

When Mr Saeed arrived, Dr Whitecross said, 'Tell Mr Ashoka what you told me in your letter.'

After Mr Saeed had repeated the contents of the letter, Dr Whitecross addressed Mr Ashoka: 'Mr Saeed is a loyal servant of the Department and the state. You have failed. Do you realise what may have happened to the flag? It may have been used to clean the floor or someone's shoes. The Department will not forget that you endangered the dignity of national property. Please submit a full statement to me on the loss of the flag.'

As the inspector was about to leave, the secretary came in with tea. Mr Ashoka invited him to stay.

'No,' he said curtly, walking out.

182

Mr Ashoka was left alone with his deputy.

'Why did you inform the inspector?'

'It was my duty.'

'Your duty was to inform me first.'

'I preferred to communicate with higher authority,' the deputy said, with an insolent nuance in his voice.

'Please have some tea,' Mr Ashoka said, as a feeling of isolation began to garotte him.

'No, thank you,' the deputy refused, walking out.

Mr Ashoka stood staring at the tea-pot and the cups, the sugar in its chrome bowl, the gleaming spoons. Both Dr Whitecross and Mr Saeed had spurned his invitation. The social offence struck home: it was more painful to bear than all the words he had heard about the flag. The tea had been his gesture of goodwill to them; its drinking was a universal ritual that affirmed the human bond. He felt himself receding away from everyone into the hermetic centre of his desolation.

CHAPTER TWENTY-SIX

The Director of Education dismissed the pleas of both the Parents' Committee and the Teachers' Association to reinstate Zenobia, with the comment that 'she was found guilty of misconduct in terms of Sections 15, 16 and 17 of the Education Act at an enquiry held in open court and, further, her punishment is in accordance with the provisions of the said Act.'

Mr Ashoka was bitterly disappointed. He had hoped that Zenobia's reinstatement would reduce the anger and hate of the community against him. Filled with depression and anxiety, he was now a much subdued man at school.

The Director's decision immediately led to the drawing up of a petition by the Parents' Committee to have Mr Ashoka dismissed. Many people assisted the Parents' Committee, and no one was more active in collecting signatures than Prince Yusuf, whose Mustang was seen moving from house to house during evenings and weekends.

While the petition was still in circulation, the pupils at

Ashoka High School decided to hold a protest demonstration. The demonstration was not only a reaction to Zenobia's dismissal, but a culmination of all that the pupils had endured during Mr Ashoka's reign, from the humiliation of the demotions to the physical anguish of the beatings. They gathered on a Saturday afternoon on a sports field. News of the demonstration had already spread and a number of teachers, parents and sympathisers joined in.

The protest was a noisy one. Placards had been made and these screamed in vermilion and orange paint: 'Down with the Oppressor!', 'Zenobia in, Ashoka out!'; 'Education, not Tyranny!'; 'Nero — Hitler — Ashoka'; 'Ashoka Rex vincit Ashoka Spurious!' (this was a variation on the school's motto: Labor vincit omnia.) A number of pupils made rhetorical speeches; newspaper reporters recorded these and took photographs.

Later, a senior pupil suggested that the demonstration should continue in front of Mr Ashoka's house. They set out.

Mr Ashoka was cloistered in his study, standing before the statuette of Krishna. His wife had gone to visit a relative and Deva was playing with friends in the street. On the previous day he had heard of the planned demonstration from his secretary. He saw clearly now what lay ahead of him: his fall, if the course of events continued. With hands pressed close he prayed fervently: for a transfer to a school in another province, for Zenobia's reinstatement, for divine intervention. As he prayed, sacrilegious wishes began to swell in his mind: for the sudden death of Zenobia, for the destruction of Lenasia by a tornado, for the devastation of Africa by an atom bomb, for the annihilation of the whole world. He wept and cried out, 'Mercy, O Lord, Mercy!' As the tears formed, each one contained a burning wick at its heart.

He heard a murmuring outside the house, then sudden shouting and the hooting of cars. He went quickly to the lounge window and from behind the nylon mesh curtain saw pupils milling in the street, waving placards. In their midst, close to the front gate, was the Mustang; sitting cross-legged on the bonnet was Eleanor in a long blue dress, her ash-blonde hair coiled above her head, a cigarette smoking in a long holder. Prince Yusuf, in a cream shirt, a patterned yellow scarf, cream pants and a dark blue double-breasted jacket, was standing beside her with folded arms. Mr Ashoka's eyes became riveted on the couple and the pupils' faces turned into an amorphous scowling blur. The accusatory placards, held aloft, dripped blood. The striking clarity with which Prince Yusuf and Eleanor appeared to Mr Ashoka seemed strangely unreal, as though what he saw before him was a picture in an art gallery. Then he saw Eleanor lift her cigarette holder to her red lips and again, as in the courtroom corridor, flick the ash disdainfully in his direction.

Deva, in green pants and yellow shirt, appeared on the lawn, and like a circus acrobat wheeled across on his hands. He then somersaulted, skipped, jumped, dived, rolled, leapt into the air and shouted out the slogans from the placards while facing his father. Deva came closer to the window — his father retreated towards the wall of the room — and laughed and made pugilistic gestures at him.

He ran to his study and bowed his head before the god. When he looked up, the brass statuette underwent a vengeful metamorphosis, turning into a hideous, angry demon. He was overwhelmed by a sense of spiritual defilement, of essential corruption.

Deva's performance was enjoyed immensely by the pupils and had the effect of reducing some of the seriousness of the protest. Slowly they began to disperse.

Mr Ashoka heard the noise receding and then there was silence. Yet the invasion of his devastated consciousness continued. He felt hostile presences closing around him and there was no one to whom he could turn. Then a brick exploded on the zinc roof of his house.

When his wife came home in the evening, he told her of the demonstration. She wept as she usually did when he told her of his troubles. He did not tell her that Deva had joined the demonstrators against him.

The evening passed into night, but Deva did not return. Husband and wife had a lonely supper, and later Mrs Ashoka went to enquire from her neighbours if they had seen her son. They said that he had gone off with the demonstrators.

It was past eleven o'clock when Mrs Ashoka suggested to her husband that he should ask the police for help. He telephoned the police and was told that they would make a search for him.

Mr and Mrs Ashoka kept vigil for Deva the entire night and despite several telephone calls to the police, who assured them that they were still searching for the boy, he was not found by the morning.

Later Mr Ashoka went to see officer Ayer. He told him of the demonstration and his belief that Deva had been kidnapped by Prince Yusuf and Eleanor. 'They may even have killed him by now,' he said. 'That man is a villain. You should see the type of women he goes around with.'

'They won't do that,' officer Ayer said, smiling faintly. 'If anyone wanted to kill Deva, they would not have taken him away in the presence of others. But I will send out a search party.'

Mr Ashoka gave Prince Yusuf's address and told the officer that Eleanor's address could be obtained from him.

He returned home and waited. In the afternoon officer Ayer telephoned to say that the police had failed to find Deva at the homes of the people he had mentioned. However, they would continue the search.

The next morning Mr Ashoka went to school and spent the entire day in his office. Several times it occurred to him that he should call an assembly and ask the pupils if they had seen Deva. But the fear that the pupils might take the opportunity to start another demonstration against him kept him in his office. He telephoned his wife and the police several times, but Deva seemed to have vanished.

At the end of the school day he remained in his office after everyone had left and brooded over the inexplicable disappearance. Had the boy lost his memory and wandered away from home? Was he dying somewhere, in the fields beyond Lenasia, of hunger and thirst? Had he been spirited away by some thugs in the pay of Prince Yusuf and were they now, with blades, poker and tongs, torturing him? Or — the thought came to him with the certainty of an apocalyptic illumination — had the god taken his son away from him because he was tainted, irredeemably tainted, in this incarnation? Yes, his beloved Deva would never return home while he existed. He would only return once his father's bad aura was no longer a presence.

He quickly entered the strong-room, looked at the distance between the top steel shelves on either side, then went to the keyboard in the secretary's office and took the keys of the woodwork centre. He went out and soon returned with a ten-foot beam. He took a chair from his office and entered the strong-room. He stood on the chair, and placed the ends of the beam on the shelves on either side. He jumped down from the chair, went to the safe, opened it and took out the flag case. He unlocked it. The rope lay neatly coiled, thin as an ornamental snake. He took the rope, stepped on to the chair again, flung the rope over the beam and made a noose. He looked at the gallows he had constructed for himself. 'You certainly have enough rope,' he heard a voice say within him. He returned to his office, sat down at his table and wrote two letters.

To his wife he wrote: 'Deva will return as soon as I have left this incarnation. Care for him for the rest of your life if you wish to gain the blessing of Lord Krishna.'

To Deva he wrote: 'I know why you left home, though you may be unaware of the divine force that took you away. I also know that you will return — as soon as my evil aura is no longer in the way. Dearest Deva, remember always that you were your father's hope.'

He put the letters into envelopes, wrote the names of his wife and son, and placed them on the table. Finally — his last official act — he placed the office keys on the table as well.

Then he entered the strong-room and pushed the heavy steel door until it closed on the light.